The Villa of the Ferromonte

LAWRENCE B. EISENBERG

cop.a

SIMON AND SCHUSTER · NEW YORK

SBN 671–21765–8
Library of Congress Catalog Card Number: 73-22332
Designed by Eve Metz
Manufactured in the United States of America

1   2   3   4   5   6   7   8   9   10

For Barbara, Mindy and Paul
and also
For Minnie, Psammo and Myra

ACKNOWLEDGMENTS

The Ferromonte ancestors, wherever they are—
and those two alchemists—
Claire Smith
and
Phyllis Grann

1

The weathered old door shivered shut, barely leaving behind
the cold air that hung from the gray December sky. The place
hadn't changed in its outlines, he thought. It still looked like a
small fortress gone to seed, only it had gone much faster in the
eight years since he'd seen it. The ancient doorman had disappeared, as had many of the lights that once made the small
lobby look, if not luxurious, at least less gloomy. Even the fake
coals in the fake fireplace were stilled. Norman knew this was
the kind of house where once something was used up or burned
out it was gone forever.

The stenciled walls were chipped and cracked on the two
landings he passed. Even in its good days Norman had never
liked this place, and he remembered in exact detail the day of
his first visit. His six-year-old eyes had taken it all in and he'd
said to his mother as they left, "Maybe a tornado will come and
take this house away to the land of Oz." And he still remembered her laugh, twenty years later. Right here on this landing.

The number 12 was now facing him on the door directly at
the top of the landing, and it seemed a little odd. He remembered the entrance as having been much farther to the right. But
doors don't move, he thought as he twisted the old-fashioned bell
that ground out a slight squeak.

In his head he heard the strains of the song his aunts used to sing to him when he was little:

How do you do, my partner?
How do you do today-ay?
We will dance in a circle ...
I will show you the way.

Now he heard the sounds of many feet dancing and a baby's giggling and realized it wasn't his memory at all. Somebody in this building was obviously entertaining a child with that same song. Appropriate, he thought.

He twisted the bell again and tried to picture little Aunt Amy, making her way quickly through the foyers of the ten rooms she shared with Aunt Elizabeth.

"Norman?" called the always cheery voice, and the door was pulled open. She looked not very different from the last time he'd seen her—that other-worldly faded beauty just a little more faded, like a precious cracked vase. He bent down to kiss her, reminded how small and frail she really was.

In her pink peignoir, covered by a worn maroon cashmere sweater, his aunt stood out like a priceless antique in an absurd setting. And now he realized he'd been right about the door being in the wrong place. By mistake he'd knocked on the back entrance and was now in the kitchen. But it was like no kitchen he'd ever seen. More like the sub-basement of a storage warehouse. There was almost no space to walk. The once airy room now featured eight chairs, no one matching another and all in various stages of disrepair; an old heavily paneled mahogany clothes closet on top of which was an eight-drawer scratched Hepplewhite dresser which just scaled the eleven-foot ceiling; a crystal china closet whose insides were covered with faded draperies; and an enormous spanking white refrigerator that seemed just about able to cope with the huge velvet armchair sitting on it. Filling out the rest of this strange enclosure was an old-fashioned gas stove with skinny legs, under which was a tremendous stack of framed paintings; two umbrella stands, one brass, the other Delft; an enameled Austrian decorative stove with a scarred enameled chimney; a mammoth carved cherry rocker on which two cats were engaged in battle while a third played with the immense brass pendulum that hung freely from a French enamel clock, next to which was a grandfather clock. On the floor two rumpled, shredded Aubusson rugs were obvious victims of the cats' claws.

"Aunt Amy, why is all this furniture piled up in here? Is the apartment being painted?"

It was as though he hadn't said anything.

"Norman, you got so big!" She hugged him. "I almost wouldn't recognize you."

"Aunt Amy, I'm twenty-six. I haven't grown since you saw me two years ago. Why is this room so cluttered?"

"All of your little curls have straightened out. Remember, you used to refer to them as 'kowies'?"

No, he didn't remember, nor did he care.

"You had the most gorgeous hair of any five-year-old we ever knew. And those blue eyes!" She rubbed his cheek and smiled.

Why was she doing this? Why did she—why did both of his aunts—always dwell on those days when he was five?

She took the package from him and tore it open. "What beautiful flowers! Peonies—out of season. They're our favorite. Elizabeth!" she sang, "wait till you see the flowers Norman brought us." She opened a dish closet above the sink, revealing an awesome display of crystal, china and glassware, all cracked or chipped. Amid this ruined finery, yawning, was a curled-up tortoise-shell cat.

"Up there, Norman, see on the second shelf, that crystal basket with the handle? Can you reach it?"

With a silent prayer that he wouldn't start an avalanche of glass, Norman grabbed hold of the piece and realized the handle was broken off. He handed the remaining portion to her.

"This will be just fine," she said, closing the door. "We always keep peonies in this."

"Aunt Amy, how can that cat breathe in there?"

She hummed as she ran water into the basket, then moved some dishes aside on one of the tables, placed it in the center and painstakingly arranged the flowers. Norman noticed droplets of water running through a large crack in the glass.

"Aunt Amy, it's leaking."

"They really are prizewinners! Norman, we could always depend upon you."

Why wasn't she answering anything he was saying?

He cleared his throat and faked a laugh. "I made a funny mistake," he said, "coming in the back door this way. I'm sorry."

"This is the front door now, Norman."

"What do you mean, the front door? And why won't you tell me why all this furniture is in here?"

Again she ignored him. "How is it we never hear from you, darling?" she said in her Princess Margaret Rose voice. And he remembered that Aunts Elizabeth and Amy always liked to think of themselves as comparable to England's two princesses—whom they had actually known. "The last time we saw you was when I was in hospital. You never ring us up."

"If you had a telephone I'd call you, Aunt Amy. I'll never understand why you had the phone taken out."

"You could ring us at our friend Pearlie's apartment. She would give us a message. You got our message last night. See how simple it was?"

Was there any point in telling her that until last night he never knew of the existence of their friend Pearlie?

"Why don't you just get a new phone and it'll be simpler?"

"We haven't had the chance, with all of our complex ailments."

"Aunt Amy, you've been without a phone for eight years."

"What an excellent memory, Norman! But what's the difference? Neither of us will last much longer." Tears began to flow. "Norman, do you know that your Aunt Amy was once beautiful?"

He hugged her. "You still are, Aunt Amy."

She clung to him for a while, then pointed to her right leg, which had been paralyzed by a stroke two years before. "Do you see how I walk? I'm a cripple. Look at my hand!"

"Aren't there exercises?"

She waved him away with her good hand. "Ah, they're no good." From her pocket she removed a small pink ball, which she held out to him. "I'm supposed to squeeze this. It's barely good for bouncing."

"Where's Aunt Elizabeth? In her room?"

She motioned with her head toward the next room. "Right inside."

"In the dining room? What's she doing in there?"

Pushing aside the worn lace curtain in the doorway, he peered into the next room. If the clutter in the kitchen was absurd, in here it was stupefying. The room was unlit, the left half entirely filled with furniture, packages and boxes piled to the ceiling. He looked at the other side of the room and could barely make out a double bed, surrounded by more furniture. In the semidarkness he saw a figure lying half on and half off the bed.

"Aunt Elizabeth?"

"Aunt Elizabeth indeed," her voice said weakly.

"Why is your bed in the dining room?" He turned back toward the kitchen. "Aunt Amy, why is the furniture all stacked up?"

"Where else could we put it, love?" asked Elizabeth.

"In the rooms where it belongs," he said. "Why are you in here instead of your bedroom?"

"*This* is my bedroom," she said.

"What about the rest of the apartment?" he asked.

"*This* is it," she answered.

"What do you mean, Aunt Elizabeth? What happened to the rest of the apartment?" He pointed toward the door in the far wall, which, he remembered, had led from the dining room to a small study. He moved toward it.

"Keep away from that door!" Elizabeth shouted.

"Will one of you please tell me what happened to the rest of the apartment?"

"Don't shout, Norman. Look at how the child gets worked

up," Elizabeth said soothingly. "It's all very simple, dear. The place was always too big for just the two of us—and became far too expensive—and so we turned the rest back to the landlord and he broke it into other apartments."

"But why didn't you get rid of some of the furniture? How can you live in this?" Again he pointed toward the closed door. "What's in there? You mean all you kept were the two rooms?"

"No, love," Elizabeth said. "We use *that* room as a storage room." *That* room, he remembered, had always been his favorite in the apartment, where he took naps and played as a child.

"This whole place is a storage room," he muttered.

"I think we can do without sarcasm!" Elizabeth said. "Now, let's all calm down."

He pushed the wall switch, lighting the one remaining bulb in the covered crystal chandelier. Against the hand-carved headboard, mostly hidden by old clothes lumped together to form pillows, he saw the face of his Aunt Elizabeth. It was turned upward and looked waxen. No, not that exactly. Rather like a photo negative tipped at a certain angle so it looks like an eerie print. The features were the same—the aquiline nose, the large hazel eyes, the pink unlined cheeks, the perfect teeth and the thick wavy head of long silver hair that came nearly to her waist. She could almost have been a double for Amy, but with a subtle difference. If Aunt Amy was porcelain, Aunt Elizabeth was marble. She was larger, taller, stronger. "Elizabeth is made of sterner stuff than the others," Grandpa Simon used to say. "Gentle Amy, Beautiful Maria and Magnificent Elizabeth" was how he'd characterized his three youngest daughters.

Magnificent Elizabeth, now faded and shrunken and prone. Elizabeth, about whom his mother had once said, "She was the least beautiful of the three of us, but she always acted as though she was the *most*. In fact, your Aunt Elizabeth has always acted as though she was the most everything." Aunt Elizabeth, who at the age of fifteen had piloted a plane solo, who in her prime led marches for women's rights before anybody thought of the word "lib," who once spent a night in prison for attacking the mayor at an election rally.

"How are you feeling, Aunt Elizabeth?"

"Ah, what's the use, love? This is the grand finale." The elegance of her voice almost belied what she was saying.

"Aunt Elizabeth," he said, "can we take you to a hospital?"

"No, I just came from hospital. They can't do anything for me. How they poked and pulled at me! I had frightful pains in my tummy, but now they're gone and I have the most incredible pains in my feet. I know what I have. They just wouldn't tell me. When I try to walk it's excruciating."

The worn silver-fox cape covering her stopped just short of her feet, which were encased in high-heeled black satin pumps.

"If your feet hurt you shouldn't be wearing shoes."

"Oh, Norman, I tried so hard to dress up and be presentable for you, but I just couldn't make it."

"Why are your legs hanging over the side of the bed?"

"Because there's no room for them *on* the bed."

No wonder, he thought. The bed was covered with old fur coats, brass-bound wooden boxes, torn leather-bound books and a high stack of movie magazines. "Let me move some of this stuff off for you."

"No! No! Just let me alone!" Then, softly, "Norman, dear, put out the light and then put out the light."

"*Othello*—act five, scene two!" Amy shouted eagerly.

"Another winner," Elizabeth called back faintly.

Norman walked up to Amy. "Aunt Amy, how long has Aunt Elizabeth been like this?"

"Why, all her life, darling. You know we've always been avid game players."

"No, I mean how long has she had this condition?"

"Since she returned from hospital—a week."

"And how long since you . . . since you gave up the rest of the apartment?"

"Oh, just after your mother passed on."

"Why didn't you ever tell me?"

Amy shrugged, then her face brightened. "I'm so delighted you're here. You can open some cans of food for the cats. It isn't easy maneuvering with just one usable arm." She pushed aside some faded silk curtains covering a cabinet next to the sink to reveal a television set, on top of which were several dozen cans of assorted cat food.

"Why do you keep the television hidden?" he asked.

From the other room came Elizabeth's feeble voice. "It's broken."

"Why don't you have it fixed?"

"What is there of any value on that imbecile machine anyway?"

Of course.

"Come back in here. Let me look at you," she called out, her voice much stronger.

"Didn't you look at me just before?" he asked, and both women began to laugh.

"Come in here, you naughty boy."

Norman switched the light on again and Elizabeth raised her ghostly head.

"You got so handsome. Just like your father. And tall." Here they go again, he thought. "Do you still play baseball all the time?"

"In warm weather, yes."

"What's the news of your brother Charlie?"

"Nothing much."

"He married into new money, of course. But, then, money never mattered to Charlie, did it? Such an intellectual. You should do as well as he. You're by far the better-looking."

"Thanks." He fidgeted.

"And how are his children?"

"They're fine, I guess. I haven't talked to him in a long time."

"How is it you've lost touch, Norman? We haven't heard from you in a year. Don't you love your aunts any more?"

"I was just explaining to Aunt Amy. If you had a telephone—"

"I heard, but you could write. A postcard, anything. You see how quickly we rang you the last time we got a letter from you."

"I guess I'm just not a letter writer, Aunt Elizabeth."

Norman walked back into the kitchen. He noticed the table was now all wet from the leaking crystal basket.

"Aunt Amy, that water is leaking out. Can't you get something else?"

She handed him the can opener, then went through the piles of china on the table and removed four plates, which was a signal for the dish closet to squeak open. Norman started. The tortoise-shell cat leaped out to stand at his feet, joining the other three cats who were purring loudly. Before he managed to get the first can open, all four animals were on the table, staring hungrily at him.

"Now, pay attention, Norman," Amy said, reminding him of a grade school teacher. She held out the first dish, a royal blue and white Wedgwood platter, cracked down the middle. "This is Roddy's. He gets an extra-large helping." Roddy, an enormous tiger-striped cat, seemed to know this. Next she handed him a Canton dish whose corner was missing. "This is for Cyril. Give him some of the liver stuff. He's very particular." Particular Cyril was an all-gray tom of spectacular beauty. "Now Albert." Albert was the closet recluse and his dish was majolica with a large hole in its side. "Last, but by no means least," Amy sang, "our little Victoria." Victoria was a pregnant calico, and in her multi-chipped Staffordshire bowl she received a mixture of the liver and the regular.

"Gee, Aunt Amy," Norman said, "can't you get them service for four in the same pattern?"

Amy laughed, then hobbled over to a bentwood hatrack, removed a feather duster and began to flit around the meager floor space, dusting away at the piles of furniture.

"Isn't it close in here for so many cats?" Norman asked, and then his attention was drawn to a scratching sound that seemed to come from behind a door next to the sink.

"What's that noise?" he asked.

"Oh, Signe is in there," said Amy, and just as she said it he noticed the word "Signe" pasted in the middle of the door, in different size letters, like a ransom note.

"Who?"

"Signe, a cat. We keep her locked up."

"Why?"

"Because she fights."

"Why don't you get rid of her?"

"Who would take her in?" Amy asked.

Sure, he thought, a logical reason for everything.

"What is that, a closet?" he asked.

"It's our pantry—was our pantry—but now it's Signe's home," Amy said. Norman opened the door and was faced with a full-length screen door on the other side. He peered into the pantry but couldn't see anything. "Shouldn't I give her some food?" he asked.

"I guess so, but be careful, she's vicious," Amy said, handing him a ruined Baccarat crystal bowl.

The screen door slammed behind him and he switched on the light. Curled up on a torn velvet cushion in the far corner of the large closet was a black cat. She mewed softly and he patted her on the head, noticing she wasn't quite all black. Tiny white worry lines furrowed her brow, and she looked at him with what seemed almost human intelligence. He shook his head. Poor caged-up animal. He picked her up and put her on the floor next to the food, which she devoured, tail wagging.

Leaving the door ajar behind him, he said to Amy, "She seems very gentle."

"Appearances are deceiving!" came the voice of Elizabeth.

"How can she breathe in there?" he asked.

"Oh, we usually leave the door open, so long as the screen door is bolted," Amy said.

"If I can find a home for Signe, do you want to give her away?" he asked.

"No, she stays here," said Elizabeth very firmly.

"But she's a prisoner, Aunt Elizabeth."

"She's— We're not going to be responsible for any damage she does to anybody else," Elizabeth said. "Besides, she was a gift and it would be rude to give her away."

"And she's brought us good luck," trilled Amy.

"Good luck!" he shouted. "What do you consider bad luck?"

Elizabeth laughed. "Amy was just teasing, dear."

"Yes," said Amy, "just teasing. Norman, I wonder whether you might do us a splendid favor and get some groceries?"

"Sure, what do you need?"

"Milk, ginger ale and Twinkies."

"Where's the nearest grocery?"

"Just next door," Amy said.

From inside came Elizabeth's voice again. "When you're in the grocery, don't tell her who you are or whom you came for."

Why would I bother? he wondered. "Is there anything else?"

"Yes, come in here, darling," Elizabeth moaned.

He went inside. "Are you in pain?"

"Excruciating."

"Do you have painkillers?"

"No. Can you get me some aspirin? A small tin—the smallest they make. I'm dying. No sense wasting them. Wait, I'll give you some money."

"I have money," he said.

"No, one thing we never accepted was charity. Amy, give him some."

Amy went to a drawer in the remains of a Chippendale desk and removed a heart-shaped enameled glass box from which she took some bills and said, "Here, little Norman," in that same voice, the voice she used to use when she handed him crisp dollar bills every time his mother took him to visit.

"Forget it," he said. He was about to go into the kitchen when he heard a noise from the locked room beyond the dining room.

"What's that?"

"Nothing, dear. Forget it," said Elizabeth.

"But I heard a noise. Maybe one of the cats is in there. Maybe I should . . ." He pushed on the door, but it wouldn't budge. It was almost as though some pressure were being applied from the other side, like a strong wind.

"Take your hands off that door!" Elizabeth shrieked in a voice she had never used to him in all his life. He stared at her. "I mean, Norman, dear, it would be dangerous for you to go in there, with all the furniture piled up so precariously. No cats are in there. It's probably a box that fell down. Ignore it."

"Aunt Elizabeth, I couldn't even get in there if I tried. The door is jammed."

Just before opening the outside door he noticed that more than half the water had leaked out of the crystal basket. But what was the point in mentioning it?

As the door was closing behind him he heard Elizabeth say, "Amy, make sure the sherry glasses are out in the drawing room for little Norman's party." No, he didn't really hear that. Yes, he did. But his memory was playing some kind of trick. He remembered in scrupulous detail the day of his fifth birthday party, given for him by Elizabeth and Amy in Grandpa Simon's mansion on upper Fifth Avenue. One of the reasons he remembered it so well was that it had been reviewed for him all through his life by his mother and her sisters. They'd used the occasion to fill the house with such an array of statesmen, Nobel Prize winners and anybody else "who mattered," that the *New York Times* had devoted a full page to it. In those days, of course, they were known as "those irrepressible Gould sisters," and one of the big amusements around "Grandpa Thimon'th cathle," as Norman used to call it, was to get little Norman to say that phrase. Well, they still were those irrepressible Gould sisters, as far as they were concerned, and what puzzled Norman the most was their almost purposeful unawareness of their surroundings.

He had his foot on the first step when he heard Amy call, "We're out of lemonade."

"Oh, dear!" Elizabeth exclaimed. "Because I know little Norman shall be wanting some."

Sure, he thought, that's all that's on little Norman's mind—drinking lemonade with his aunties in a room filled with piled-up furniture and faded drapes.

2

He raced down the stairs and into "Berkenblitt's Bargains," idly glancing at the holly wreath in the window with the "Peace on Earth—Now!" in ornate gold letters around its rim. Then his eyes lit on the proprietress and he almost gasped. She was one of those people who looked totally foreign to her surroundings —like a taxi driver with an Oxford accent or an elevator operator with a classic Greek profile. Except she would have been foreign to any surroundings, especially those of a shabby, dimly lit grocery store that was as long—and almost as narrow—as a bowling alley. No, thought Norman, there was one place where she would fit—as housekeeper in a mansion on the lonely moors of Scotland, or playing Mrs. Danvers in a road company of *Rebecca.* Probably in her late fifties, though she appeared ancient. Her face was skeletal, the skin pulled tightly back, with deep frown lines that looked as though they had been cut into it. It was covered with heavy, almost white powder, the eyes slanted by mascara and shaded by frighteningly long lashes. The shiny black hair was pulled back tightly into a bun, and she was wearing a full-length black woolen dress with a locket on a ribbon around her neck.

She raised her eyebrow and glanced at him in what seemed a deliberate attempt to be mysterious. But Norman didn't feel like laughing, because there was *something* about her, something vaguely threatening. She seemed to be studying him.

"May I help you, young man?" If her looks were strange, her voice was even stranger. Overly elegant, like somebody trying to disguise an accent.

He ticked off his small list. As soon as he got to the Twinkies, her eyelashes flickered and she gave him a sidelong glance, then asked in a hushed tone, "How is she?"

"Who?"

"Miss Gould, of course." She smiled conspiratorially.

"How'd you know this was for her?"

He wouldn't have been surprised if she'd batted those terrible lashes and said. "Why I know *everything,* young man," but he was more shocked at what she did say: "I recognized you, of course. You haven't changed."

He looked at her curiously and she gave him that sidelong glance again. Without wanting to be rude, he couldn't prevent himself from asking, "Do I know you?"

"I guess you might say I know you," she said, smiling very slightly.

He felt like leaving the store without waiting for his groceries, then reminded himself how idiotically he was behaving. Of course she knew him. All those times his mother had brought him to visit Elizabeth and Amy when he was young. Still, this wasn't the kind of person you forgot.

Now she took his hand. Hers felt like a piece of dry ice—cold and burning—and he wanted to pull away but was afraid of offending her.

"Did they ever show you their house uptown?" she asked with an all-knowing smile, and he wished she would just give him his order and shut up. He was too old for this I-remember-you-when-you-were-little routine from a stranger. But not too old, obviously, to be irrationally frightened.

And what an odd way to ask that question.

"Yes," he answered. "Since it was my grandfather's house, I was there often."

She pulled her lips in and released his hand. "I was there once," she said, looking off into an imaginary distance, "but your aunts never invited me again." She turned her face in profile, as if punctuating her remark.

"Oh," he said, thinking it was a stupid response.

Now she turned back to him and he saw total hatred in her eyes. "Ask them"—she smiled, opening her mouth wide to reveal teeth that looked as though they'd been sharpened—"why they never invite Natalie to see them any more."

"Sure," he said, trying to control his voice. "May I have my order now?"

She gave him another sidelong glance, then broke into a calculated laugh that sounded like Hmm, hmm, hmm. "The same pretensions as the old ladies, eh?" The odd laugh followed him out.

He raced up the stairs and was about to bang on the door, when he heard loud waltz music, then Aunt Elizabeth's voice.

"Amy"—she laughed—"I've come to the conclusion that dancing alone is the only way to protect your toes."

"Well, take care, Lizbeth! You'll ruin your new dress."

He twisted the bell. Silence. He twisted again.

"Who is it?" called Amy.

"Me, Norman. Open up."

"Be a good boy, Norman, and don't be impatient," she shouted and then swung the door open.

"What do you mean, 'Be a good boy, Norman'? And why were you and Aunt Elizabeth talking that way?"

"What way?"

"You said something about her dress and I heard loud music—"

"Oh." Amy giggled. "You must have heard the radio of the people upstairs. They're deaf and like to play it loud."

"Come on, I'm not crazy, Aunt Amy. I heard you and Aunt Elizabeth talking like you used to talk."

"What do you mean, 'like you used to talk,' Norman?" Elizabeth called. "We've always talked like we used to talk. Did you get me the aspirin?"

He stared at her through the lace curtain. Nothing had changed. O.K., they're getting senile, or he was hallucinating. In a place like this, if that was the most that could happen to him, it was O.K.

He got some water from the sink, ignoring the mew of the

cat curled up in the dish drain, and went into the dining room with the aspirins.

"I only want one," Elizabeth moaned.

"Take two. One isn't going to help you."

"I know only too well what's going to help me, young man. Do you think I'm incapable of making a decision?"

He watched her grimace as she chewed the aspirin and finally gulped down the water. He supposed it was useless to tell her she could avoid the ugly taste if she just swallowed it, but one just never told Aunt Elizabeth what to do.

"You were certainly right about not talking to that Natalie down there," he said. "And she looks just like—"

"What!" Elizabeth exclaimed. "How'd you know her name?"

"She told it to me."

She got furious. "Didn't I warn you not to tell her who you were? Why did you disobey me?"

"I didn't. She knew me. Aunt Elizabeth, I guess she saw me when my mother brought me here, but, well—"

Amy began to moan from the kitchen, and Norman rushed in. She was standing in the middle of the room, face buried in the feather duster.

"What's wrong, Aunt Amy?"

"Nothing!" Elizabeth shouted in. "Nothing is wrong with her. She has these little spells. Amy, how do you like that—baggage!"

"She said one thing that was odd," he said. "That she'd been to the big house uptown, and I should ask you why you don't invite her to visit you any more."

"Can you believe that gall?" Elizabeth said. "That witch! Oh, perhaps I shouldn't have said that."

"Aunt Elizabeth, forgive me, but why would you ever have invited her to the house uptown? And where did you know her from?"

Elizabeth gasped so loud he thought she was having a heart attack. "More water," she moaned.

"Let me tell you something," she said after gulping down the water, all of the old command returning to the voice. "Scum always rises to the top." She gave a long sigh. "When you were very little and we still lived uptown in our real house we felt sorry for her because her sister was one of our maids, and we invited her to have tea with us in the garden. And she behaved . . . well, she behaved like a person of her sort behaves." She laughed. "I guess I took care of her though, Amy?" she called out.

"You certainly did," Amy shouted back.

"What did you do?" Norman asked.

"Why, we never invited her again, that's what we did," Elizabeth said triumphantly.

What a pointless story, he thought.

"Isn't it a funny coincidence that you should live right next door to her store after all these years," he said.

"Yes, isn't it?" Elizabeth snapped majestically. "But we just buy our merchandise and have no truck with her otherwise."

I suppose, he mused, it would be useless to ask why they didn't just buy in another store.

"What's her background?" Norman asked. "I mean, that melodramatic accent and that creepy dress."

Elizabeth just stared at him. "Aunt Elizabeth?"

"Yes?" she said musically.

"What's Natalie's background?"

"I'm sure I wouldn't want to know, she snapped.

His eyes were drawn to the bed. "Aunt Elizabeth, why isn't there a sheet on here?"

"Because! That's why!"

"Let me buy you a sheet."

"Must you be a bad boy? I have twenty-five brand-new silk sheets packed away. Daddy got them as a gift from the Emperor—"

"Then why don't you tell me where they are? I'll get one out and make the bed for you."

"No, child, it's too complicated to get at them." Then, almost to herself, she mumbled, "They're far too nice for this little pied-à-terre. It's so ghastly camping out like this."

"What? What did you say?" he asked.

"Nothing, Norman," she said almost inaudibly. "They say that when you're dying you begin to ramble."

"How do you know you're dying, Aunt Elizabeth? Did a doctor tell you?"

"There are some things you don't have to be told. Ah, what's the use of talking? We Goulds—we are such stuff as dreams are made on."

"*The Tempest*—Act three, scene three," Amy shouted in. "Also Humphrey Bogart's last line in *The Maltese Falcon!*"

She's dying and playing games, Norman thought as he walked back into the kitchen. He noticed the grocery bag was still on the table. "Let me put your milk away," he muttered.

"You can't," Amy said.

He opened the refrigerator. Its insides were spotlessly clean and neatly filled with books and small pieces of china.

"There's no room for the milk."

Then, just as Amy said, "Well, we don't keep food in there. It's broken," he realized the refrigerator wasn't cold.

He slammed the door shut. "Why don't you have it fixed?" He knew the question was pointless.

"Don't fret over it, darling. We just haven't had the time to devote to these matters."

"How do you keep your food cold?"

"We keep it on the windowsill," she said proudly, like a child displaying her room to an adult. "And we keep milk in a pan of cold water on the sink." Now she almost trilled. "It's all very simple." Then she picked up the feather duster once again and began to flick it around.

I can't take this any more, he thought, and walked back into the dining room. "Aunt Elizabeth, may I talk to you for a minute? Seriously?" he asked softly. She nodded and he took her cold, moist, bony hand. "What can I do to convince you to get rid of some of this furniture or to move out of here? The neighborhood has gone—"

"We're not moving, and that's final!" she said curtly.

"O.K., O.K. Will you let me come in and straighten this place out for you? Get rid of some of the debris? I'll paint it and I'll buy you new curtains."

"New curtains? After seeing what's hanging on our windows you want to get us new curtains? That's too funny. Are you aware, Norman, of the origin of the curtain between these two rooms? Take another look at it."

He glanced at the shredded lace.

"That is handmade Belgian lace, designed for and given to your grandmother by the King of Belgium. Your Grandpa Simon wanted to bury it with her, but I wouldn't hear of it."

"Yes, Aunt Elizabeth, I can certainly understand why. But I'd just like to bring some order in here, put the furniture around where you can get at it. Buy you a new refrigerator. I'll get you one for Christmas. At least let me do that. You can't live like . . . like a pair of stuffed owls in a junk shop."

"Stuffed owls!" she shouted. "Did you hear our nephew, Amy? Do you have any idea, young man, of the background from which you come?" Here it comes again, he thought. "Do you know that we lived in the finest house in London? That the Prince of Wales was a frequent visitor even after Daddy forced us to move to New York? Do you remember your fifth birthday party, Norman? Or our house? You certainly should. And don't you forget we moved to New York in 1929, and during the entire Depression we still lived like royalty. Better! Ah, what's the use? All gone, all gone. Daddy gave it away, the lawyers took it away. We couldn't manage it. What did we know about managing money?" She started to cry.

"Didn't you get a lot of money for the house? Don't you still get money?"

"Norman, don't worry so much about us," said Elizabeth.

"Don't worry so much!" he said, "I don't understand you. You have practically no money to live on—and all this furniture. There must be some of it that's still worth something. I can try to sell it for you."

"We don't need any more money!" she said. "Our needs are simple. Won't you understand? There are more important things." She began to cough violently.

"Aunt Elizabeth, would you like a doctor?"

"No, I'm beyond doctors. Norman, dear, do you think you can get me some painkillers?"

"Well, I haven't seen a doctor in four years. I don't—"

"Amy," she called out, "get the Fabergé egg."

In an instant Amy was in the room holding a chipped and dented enamel egg standing on a broken base of semiprecious stone. She pressed something and the front of the egg opened to reveal a crumpled piece of lined composition paper, which she handed to Elizabeth, who unfolded and scanned it.

"Here," Elizabeth said, pointing at the paper, "there's a Dr. Wasserman on East Eighteenth Street. Go ring him."

"With what? If you had a phone—"

"Why do you keep nagging me about a phone? How long will I be here anyway?"

"O.K., O.K."

"He treated me for diabetes five years ago. Call him—don't tell him who you are—and offer him five dollars for some painkillers."

"Oh, sure, Aunt Elizabeth, in a neighborhood full of junkies I'll call a strange doctor and offer him money for painkillers. No doctor is going to give me—"

Her voice got much stronger and now he remembered something his mother had told him when he was very young: "When Elizabeth talks, people listen."

"How do you know, my doubting boy?" she asked. "The language has far too many negatives in it. The truly great don't know the meaning of the word."

"Well," he said, "maybe I can call the doctor I used last. I don't know. I'm going home now."

"Splendid!" Amy said, and he looked at her curiously. "I mean, Norman, don't you have to go to work?"

"No, I took the day off. I'll come back later if— I'll call my doctor and see if he'll give me a prescription. If I don't . . ."

He began to wonder why he couldn't finish a sentence.

"Very well, Norman, you're a fine boy. Isn't he, Amy?"

"A fine boy," Amy echoed.

On his way to the front door he noticed that the water from the crystal basket was all gone. Amy stood near the stove staring at him.

"Aunt Amy, the peonies are out of water," he said quietly.

"Dear me, the thirsty devils, I'll have to get them some more," she said as the door closed behind him.

He stood outside quietly, then pressed his ear to the door. Not a sound. He checked his watch. Four minutes went by. Then the strains of music began. It was an opera, the full orchestral sounds leaping out at him. He looked toward the ceiling to see whether it was coming from the floor above.

Then, in the voice he remembered from his childhood, he heard Elizabeth: "That's one of the more boring theories I've heard this year. On what holy tablet is it written that the sex drive is the exclusive province of men? It was Eve, after all, who had the apple first!"

"Lizbeth!" said Amy. "Sometimes you go too far for even *you*. Look at Maria. She's blushing!"

A lot of laughter followed, then more music, all-consuming music. Norman ran down the stairs and up the street as fast as he could go. Maybe running would straighten out his head. Sure, the neighbor's opera music was too loud. Sure, they played word games and lived in the past in a strangling, faded clutter of cracks and chips and mustiness. But why had Amy said, "Look at Maria. She's blushing!" when Maria, his mother, had been dead for eight years?

3

He remembered nothing about the subway trip home, and he took deep breaths as his elevator raced up to the nineteenth floor, hoping he could force his way back to some kind of reality. He'd been down at his aunts' place only a couple of hours, but it seemed as though they had spanned his whole life. Well, as a matter of fact they had. Little Norman. Little Norman and his curls.

Before he could get his door completely open, he heard the "Mow" of Fulcho, his cat, who strolled out into the corridor, attached himself with both paws to Norman's left ankle, and let Norman drag him into the apartment.

"I forgot I had a cat at home," he said to Fulcho as he turned on the light. "I just saw five others—two of them were in mortal combat on a rocker, the third is pregnant, the fourth sleeps in a closet with cracked crystal and the fifth is in jail. Do you care, Fulcho?"

The alert three-year-old Siamese eyes stared at him. Norman scooped him off the floor and rubbed noses with him. "Fulcho, there are actually times I appreciate you, despite your rotten disposition." He made to rub noses again and Fulcho protected his face by pushing Norman away with both dark brown paws.

"O.K.," he said, "maybe you'd rather live with my aunts downtown. You'd have lots of company there." He tossed Fulcho onto the couch and the cat made a perfect landing, then curled up against a blue pillow.

"Just remember," Norman said, "that you're my cat by default." Very funny, he thought, and he found himself, after three years, still smarting. Because Fulcho was the surprise wedding gift Norman had bought for Linda two days before they were scheduled to be married. One day before, Linda disappeared and left him with a short note, whose contents he could reel off in his sleep.

Dearest Norman,

I always said you were too good for practically anybody—especially me—and you always thought I was kidding. Well, I have to bow out and I haven't the courage to tell you why, now. But I want you to know you're the finest person I've ever known—you really *are* Prince Norman. And I'm truly sorry.

Love,
Linda

Months later Norman found out what she was sorry about, not from Linda but from overhearing Brad Horowitz in the office telling his friend Max O'Hara that all the time they'd been engaged Linda had been seeing someone else.

Two and a half years since this overheard conversation, and he still trembled. Why, Norman, he asked himself, did you go on working in that place where you met Linda? Why didn't you mop up the floor with Max and Brad? Why have you allowed these same two to get away with leaving you little notes and practical jokes over the years to remind you of Linda? Because, Norman, he answered, that's the way you are. Throughout his life he'd been disappointed in people, and his mother would always explain: "That's because, my darling, I've brought you up to expect only the best out of life." And Mother had also taught him to "rise above it, because that's what a Gould does." Too bad his father wasn't around enough to teach him what a Dickens did. So he not only rose above everything, but each time he did somebody laughed at him, because people just didn't do that kind of thing. Which prompted the various nicknames he sometimes couldn't help overhearing: Prince Norman, H.H. (His Highness).

He sighed and stared at Fulcho.

"Mrrr," said the cat, his word for hungry.

Norman placed his dish on the floor and Fulcho plunged in.

"I bet you wouldn't love me so much if I didn't give you kidneys," he said, smiling and walking to the window to inspect his Wandering Jew plant. He broke off four dead leaves and watered it.

The phone rang. "Norman, hi, it's Sharon." Sharon worked in his office. She liked him and he liked her, but not the way Sharon wanted him to like her.

"Norman, they told me you had a virus, so I called to see how you were feeling. I called a lot of times today. Weren't you answering the phone?"

Idiot, he thought, can't even steal a day off convincingly.

"Uh, I just turned the phone off so I could sleep."

"Well, how are you, Norman?"

"Oh, I'm better, I guess."

"Well, take care of yourself. You mean a lot to all of us around here. In a secret poll today the girls on the fourteenth floor voted you the man they know least and like best."

"Thanks."

Well, he thought, the winner of another popularity contest. But Norman had always won contests with girls, and very early in life he realized all he ever had to do was just let nature take its course. It was part of being a Gould, be guessed. Things and people were just attracted to you. But, being a Gould, he had never committed himself until Linda, and when she'd disappeared he'd never really gotten over it. He smiled now as he remembered the period immediately following that Brad-Max conversation —a period of one month when he'd had a different girl for each of the thirty-one nights, and then he hadn't touched another one for three months. And since then only occasionally. It was imitation love, he'd decided. And anything real, well, he couldn't cope with anything real. That's why he was putting off Sharon.

He stared out the windows at the park. It was already dark and only five o'clock. Fulcho leaped up onto the windowsill, leaned against the glass and peered out.

"Nice view, huh, Fulcho? Would anybody believe old Norman would luck onto a view like this?" Blind luck. He'd been looking at another apartment in the building, referred by somebody in his office, and was just about to sign the paper committing himself to payment of $3000—which was little more than a bribe—when the prospective sellers, astonished at his willingness to pay without protest or bargaining, decided to raise the price to $4000. He'd said he'd have to check the bank about a loan.

On the way down in the elevator he'd run into a busybody old lady, with her companion, who wanted to know why he was looking so glum. And he had told her. Mrs. Shomer turned out to be a fairy godmother. She told him that her friend Verna, who lived in the studio apartment next door, was in a bad way in the hospital and might be willing to sublet to him. If he hadn't been so shy he'd have kissed her. Well, Verna signed a sublet contract with Norman from her hospital bed and left the world five weeks later. And Norman got the apartment, with the furniture. But he'd disposed of the pieces and bought all new things as a surprise for Linda. How lucky, he'd thought at the time, that the furniture arrived four days before the wedding.

One of the things he liked best about Mrs. Shomer was that she never asked what had happened to the bride who was supposed to share the apartment. Well, he'd returned the favor during those three years by doing frequent odd jobs for her. There was a handyman in the building, but Mrs. Shomer preferred Norman to do the work because, she said, he did it with love. Sometimes she'd have her companion, Ellen, knocking at his door at six o'clock in the morning if the light bulb was out in her refrigerator. But, Norman figured, who else would have gotten him a large studio apartment in the Sixties facing Central Park for $110 a month? He never told anybody about the bargain, because he didn't want to hear "Money goes to money" one more time in his life.

He opened the refrigerator and poured himself a glass of champagne. A habit that would probably add fuel to his Prince Norman image. He drank champagne every night of his life now, knocking off about two bottles a week. It made the evening shorter. He still had two goblets left from his mother's good crystal set—whose cracked mates he'd noticed at Elizabeth and Amy's this afternoon—and every night he offered Fulcho a snort in one of them and every night the cat ignored him.

Champagne had been the favored drink of "those Gould sisters," especially his mother. To the point that one year ago, on his twenty-fifth birthday, an attorney notified him that his mother, dead seven years, had left him a $5000 trust fund, effective immediately, but stipulating that the money be spent only on champagne.

He ran his finger into the indentations in the crystal. Those Gould sisters, how could they stand to live this way after what they'd had? He thought about the house on Fifth Avenue, and the many times his mother had taken him to visit Grandpa Simon and Aunts Elizabeth and Amy in their big beautiful garden. Strains of that song he'd heard this afternoon came back to him from right out of the past. Now he wondered whether he'd really heard it from some other apartment, because his mind was playing so many tricks today. Had Amy really said, "Look at Maria, she's blushing"? Or if Aunt Amy hadn't said it, why had he heard it at all?

He poured a second glass of champagne, then put it down and went to his junk closet, where—after rummaging through a box containing old baseball cards, letters and an ivory-bound New Testament which was a gift from Elizabeth and Amy on some birthday—he located "Our Family Album." On the first page: "The Gould Sisters in Their Garden on a Lovely Spring Day, London, 1927." Pictures of Elizabeth and Amy, ages twenty-one and nineteen, in their corseted, grown-up silks, with "baby sister Maria"—his mother, age fifteen—in a diminutive version of the finery her older sisters wore. All had the "Gould Sisters' Trademark"—sparkling "saucer eyes" and what Norman's mother used to refer to as "titian hair."

On the next page was Aunt Elizabeth's wedding picture, September 4, 1928, long before Norman was born, so he never got the chance to call Lorenzo Ferromonte "uncle," because Elizabeth received a mysterious annulment in less than a year and nobody had ever heard from the bridegroom afterwards. Every time Norman had asked about it he was told, "Mind your business." One day—when he was twelve and they thought he was asleep in that little den that was now the back room of their nightmare apartment—he heard his mother and her sisters talking about it. And it wasn't until years later that he figured it out. Uncle Renzo's disappearance immediately followed Aunt Elizabeth's discovery of her groom in bed with a boy. Norman laughed. There was nobody around to tell him it wasn't nice to laugh at such things.

The next page featured more of the wedding, one of the most grandiose affairs of 1928. It seems Simon Gould, Norman's grandfather and father of Elizabeth, Amy and Maria, was one of the first of the big spenders. He flew the whole of his London family to Rome to hold the wedding in the garden of the Ferromonte estate on the old Appian Way. Never one to deny his family anything, as soon as Simon had been told by Elizabeth that she'd fallen in love on holiday with an Italian of noble descent, he took off immediately for Rome, negotiated with the Ferromonte family and the date was set. And the three youngest Gould sisters spent the remainder of the summer on the estate. After the annulment the disgrace was such that Simon felt a channel was not enough to separate his family from the Ferromontes. Only an ocean would do, and he moved everybody to New York.

In the background of one of the pictures, Norman saw four more of Grandpa Simon's children—aunts and uncles he'd never met: Aunt Andrea (dead two years later of tuberculosis), Aunt Roberta (who died in an insane asylum in 1931), Uncle

Michael (who died of leukemia in 1932), and Uncle Edgar (who took his own life in 1934). Norman's mother used to tell him that she and her surviving sisters were convinced the family had been cursed by Grandpa Simon's first wife, whom he'd deserted in Russia when he ran off to England to seek his fortune and a brand-new family.

On the next page the photos of his father began. The groom's orphaned cousin from Sicily, seventeen-year-old Pietro Maori Dickens—produced by the one-night stand of a mislaid, as it were, cockney soldier and a wayward virgin—now spending a holiday at the Ferromonte mansion, was photographed with the wedding party. Grandpa Simon had taken such a fancy to the boy that he requested, and got, the Ferromontes' permission to adopt him and take him back to England to live. Simon's fondness even extended to giving the hand of his youngest daughter, Maria, to her adopted brother. Well, whatever the curse from the Russian first wife, it wasn't transferred to stepchildren. Pietro Maori Dickens, gifted by the gods and his parents' genes with unbelievable good looks, led a life that was more than charmed. After he divorced Norman's mother when Norman was six, he went on to a series of successful liaisons with rich New York ladies. Was it only a coincidence that the divorce had occurred just six months after Simon Gould's death, when the real money had stopped coming? During Simon's lifetime, Norman had been told, his financial gifts to Maria and Pietro had been lavish. After his death, when attorneys and financial wizards finished picking the bones, all that was left, it seemed, was the house and its furnishings and various trust funds—enough to insure that Elizabeth and Amy and Maria and her family would have roofs over their heads and that Norman and Charles would be guaranteed first-rate education. But there was very little else. No more servants. No more large Fifth Avenue apartment. Pietro Maori Dickens, it was assumed, was going to have to go out and work. And Pietro obviously didn't like the idea at all. How many times have I seen him since I was six? Norman wondered. Probably less than twenty, the last of which was Pietro Maori

Dickens' funeral ten years ago. Do I look like him? No, more like my mother. But not like her either. He remembered his father in the casket, most of the flamboyant good looks still in the waxen figure created by the embalmers.

The next page was another picture of the wedding reception, with all participants posing against some old Roman ruins. "The New Couple on the Old Appian Way." And a shot of Pietro, alone and astonishingly handsome, against a field of wild poppies. "Pietro's Beginnings," Maria had written, "Before He Became Our Brother—And Long Before He Became My Husband and Nipped My Non-Existent Acting Career in the Bud."

Norman slammed the book shut. Poor old Mother, who needed to be reminded of past glories, of money that had been spent, of lives that had been wasted.

He went back to his champagne and heated up a Mexican TV dinner, wishing he'd never been summoned to see Amy and Elizabeth, then feeling guilty, because all through his life he had loved these aunts so much. They weren't just aunts, more like extensions of his mother. But he'd grown away from them. It was natural, being away at Princeton and then Vietnam and then just the momentum of being away from them. Still it was odd that he had never been to their house since the day of his mother's funeral eight years ago. But that wasn't entirely his fault. Every time he'd wanted to visit, Aunt Elizabeth had offered some excuse: "The place is a mess." "Why should you make the trip downtown, when we can meet you in a nice restaurant?" "We'd much rather visit in *your* house." Communication was limited anyway, because they'd had the phone disconnected just after the funeral. He shut his eyes and tried to imagine them as they used to be—then he realized he was no different than they in treating him as though he were still five years old. Was Elizabeth really dying? he wondered. And if she was, would he have to endure the whole thing until the bitter end? Of course he would, because there was nobody else and that's why Pearlie Gish had called him last night.

"Hello, is this Norman Dickens?" she'd said in her creaky

little voice, introducing herself. "I called to tell you that the lady who used to come in and take care of your aunts died a month ago. I've been trying to help them out, but I can't do it alone, and now Elizabeth is very sick and thinks she's dying and would like to see you. Can you come down tomorrow?"

"What's wrong with her?" Norman had asked.

"I'm not sure, but she's in awful pain, and it would be a nice thing if you came to see her. They tell me they were very close to you when you were a child."

O.K., Miss Gish, I know. I would have come anyway.

Her message aroused Norman, for the first time since he'd gone to work for the company, to call in sick and go downtown to see the remains of the Gould family. The whole damn Gould family, he reflected, except for his brother, ends up with two "stuffed owls in a junk shop" and one twenty-six-year-old man who talks to his cat and drinks champagne alone. And why shouldn't I talk to my cat? he mused. It beats talking to most people.

He glanced over at Fulcho, now snoozing draped over the telephone, and realized he'd have to do what he'd been avoiding —call the doctor he hadn't seen in four years and ask him for a prescription for painkillers. He edged the receiver away from Fulcho's stomach. Disdainfully, the disturbed cat leaped from the counter to the top of the refrigerator, where he settled in as Norman dialed the doctor's number.

"Dr. Stiller's office," the service answered.

"Hello, my name is Norman Dickens and I'm a patient of Dr. Stiller's—"

"I'm sorry, Mr. Dickens," said the voice reproachfully, "but Dr. Stiller passed away last week."

Norman slammed the phone down and, with still eleven minutes to go before it was done, yanked the TV dinner from the oven and threw it onto the table.

"Fulcho," he said, "Dr. Stiller died last week. But he's so busy he still has an answering service. He's just the man for Aunt Elizabeth." He stuck his fork disgustedly into the lukewarm tacos. Then he remembered that in his medicine cabinet was a half-full bottle of empirin compound with codeine, given to him by his dentist six months ago for a toothache.

"See, Fulcho," he said, "when you're a Gould there's always a silver lining." He got the pills, then put on his navy cashmere sweater and sheepskin coat. On the way to the subway the face of Signe, the poor imprisoned cat in the pantry, flashed in his head, and he stepped into the nearest delicatessen and bought some sliced turkey for her.

He walked down the dismal street, past the dim grocery store, trying to avoid the cryptic smile of that woman staring out through its window, and rushed up the stairs.

"Who is it?" Amy called.

The Duke of Edinburgh, who do you think? "It's me."

He heard Amy's hobbling and a click as she unlocked the door, and some more hobbling. But the door was still closed. He swung it open and saw his two aunts seated over a sausage pizza at the less broken of the two kitchen tables, both clad in creased gray-blue military uniforms with visored hats.

"What *is* this?" he asked.

Elizabeth laughed. "Oh, Norman, you shock so easily. Amy and I were reminiscing before about our wartime days in the A.W.V.S.—that's American Women's Voluntary Services, and we thought, wouldn't it be fun for Norman to see us as we were? Relax, Normie, we're not as balmy as all that!" She took a large wedge of pizza from its box and began to chew on it.

"How did you get out of bed?" Norman asked her.

"Oh, that was quite a ceremony," she said. "This angel"— she motioned imperiously at Amy—"helped me."

"I brought you some painkillers," he said, handing her the vial of pills.

She broke into a smile. "I knew my little Norman would come through after all."

"I wish you'd let me get a doctor for you," he said. "These pills won't do you any good."

The hauteur of the old Aunt Elizabeth surfaced again.

"They'll do me as much good as I want them to do. But Norman, love, I haven't the strength to sit up any more. Please help me back to bed."

As he covered her with one of the furs she moaned, "Norman, come over here. I have something to tell you."

"Can't you just tell me?"

"No, I want it to be our little secret. Go over to the radio against the wall."

He noticed a curved-top radio, model circa 1935.

"Does this work?" he asked.

"No, of course not. Turn it around. Inside the back you'll see a paper bag. Fetch it for me, love."

Norman handed her the large bulging bag.

"Now," she said, smiling, "I have a surprise for you." Her slim fingers reached inside, and she pulled out a smaller paper bag from which she undid a rubber band. "Here," she said, handing it to him. "This is full of American quarters, every one of them minted the year I was born. Count out forty. I want you to have ten dollars because you've been a good boy. And you must know how sick I really am if I'm giving away my age."

My legacy, he thought. "O.K., I've got forty."

"Now put them away in your pocket. Hide them." She pulled out another small brown bag, undid several rubber bands, reached inside and removed a crumbling piece of tissue paper. From it she took something that sparkled, and she handed it to him. It was a diamond stickpin.

"This once belonged to your Grandpa Simon. Oh, it was so long ago. He was always so good to you."

He nodded.

"Not to mention how good he was to your father—both rest in peace, of course. Pietro Dickens was the handsomest man who ever lived, but he never worked a day in his life. Isn't it a beautiful pin? It has quite a history. It was his and I want it to be yours, and don't ever sell it"—her voice dropped several octaves—"because if you do, there'll be a curse on you!"

"A curse?"

She laughed. "Norman, darling, can't an old aunt have a few idiosyncrasies? We have so little, Amy and I, just each other and the bit of fun we can get out of our day-to-day existence."

Of course, fun.

"By the way, Norman, do you happen to know whether your brother still has the lamp I gave him right after your mother's death?"

"I don't know."

"It was so exquisite. A wisteria lamp. Louis C. Tiffany made it for Father. I hope Charles hasn't parted with it. Do you still have the gold hairbrush I gave you when you got out of the Army?"

Somewhere at the bottom of his junk closet. "Oh, yes, of course, Aunt Elizabeth. Well, I think I'll be going."

"Norman, precious, when you come to see us tomorrow . . ." Who told her I was coming tomorrow? he thought. ". . . I want you to bring us some things. My neighbor Pearlie upstairs does most of the shopping for us now, but she's going away for a day or so. Amy!" she called, "give him the list!"

Amy handed Norman a crumpled piece of paper on which, in a flowery handwriting, was

One midget salami
2 boxes crackerjacks
2 bags potato chips
2 boxes chocolate chip cookies
Oreos
Large jar peanut butter
Planters cashews—2 bags

"Aunt Elizabeth, shouldn't you be eating more nourishing foods in this condition?"

"Food! Glorious food!" she murmured, "Hot sausage and mustard."

"Well," Norman said, trying to stop himself from shaking his head, "I'll try to get here tomorrow."

"We're depending on you, child," said Elizabeth.

"It would be easier to depend on me if you had a telephone."

"Norman, of what use will a phone be to me in the grave? Now stop teasing. We don't need one."

"O.K. So long. I hope—"

"Well, now, young man, doesn't the shell of an old aunt get a kiss?"

Norman kissed the two faded faces, then pulled his coat on, and on the way out, on a hunch, he pushed the unlock button on the door.

Out in the hall, he heard Elizabeth call, "Amy, my love, did you finish that last box of pretzels?"

"Why would you want pretzels just before a big meal?" Amy asked. "The others will be insulted if you have no appetite!"

Elizabeth's scornful laugh followed. "Oh, Amy, the others aren't smart enough to *recognize* an insult!"

Silence. Were they really going to eat another meal after that pizza?

Well, what was the sense in even wondering. Those irrepressible Gould sisters pretty much did as they pleased.

4

Norman waited outside the door for eight minutes and didn't hear a sound. He was about to leave when he remembered the bag of turkey in his pocket.

Very quietly he pushed open the door. On one of the tables

were the four cats, who began to meow as soon as they spotted him.

"Aunt Elizabeth? Aunt Amy?" he called. No answer. Asleep, he guessed.

He unlocked the screen door on the pantry, turned on the light and stepped in.

Signe mewed gently, her intelligent eyes scanning him and, as before, he had to remind himself this was a cat.

"Signe," he said, "I brought you something for Christmas. Just don't tell the other cats."

Signe leaped off her cushion and almost bit through the wrapping before Norman got the turkey into her dish.

Just before closing the door behind her, he noticed she interrupted her ravenous eating to gaze at him once more with that human look.

He walked over to the dining room, pushed the lace curtain aside and tiptoed in, careful to avoid the various furniture legs. The old fur coats were all piled up on the bed and it was quiet. He wondered whether they'd taken off those ridiculous uniforms, and he was about to go back into the kitchen when he sniffed something. Incense. And the smell was getting stronger. He peered down at the bed and could see no movement. From the kitchen the cats seemed to be meowing in chorus. The smell of incense was very strong now and he stared at the locked door in front of him, then walked over and pushed on it. It swung open. Funny, he thought, how tightly it was locked this afternoon.

The smell was overpowering now, but he could see nothing in the room. He walked in, holding his hands out to guide him. In front of him he felt something rough, tangled. Like a bush or branches of a tree. What in God's name? he thought. Are they saving old Christmas trees? He felt something thorny strike his face and he tried to push it aside. The smell was not incense, he realized, but lilies of the valley. The far-off sounds of the cat chorus in the kitchen came back to him as he pushed his way clear of the last branch.

And then he went insane.

Before him was a rolling green meadow filled with rows of flowers of every description. Situated on guard around the flower-beds were marble statues of Venuses and gods and marble benches. A few hundred yards ahead was a pond on which sailed four swans. And just beyond the pond was a palace. The scent of lilies was still in the air, mingled with jasmine and all the sweet smells of summer. And the sounds he heard were no longer the sounds of yowling cats, but of singing summer birds. Now he heard laughter coming from the house, and a group of young people raced out shouting at one another. They were wearing costumes from the 1920s and dancing gaily toward him. And, he realized, they were talking Italian. But he couldn't make out what they were saying.

He hid behind the leafiest portion of the bush as the people got closer. So this is what happens when you die, he thought. Did I have a heart attack? Am I lying on the floor of Elizabeth and Amy's storage room? Who's going to take care of them now? Something caught his eye and he looked down and gasped. He was no longer wearing his sheepskin coat and corduroy trousers, but was dressed in a beige silk suit. Well, at least I went to heaven, he thought. I don't think hell looks like this. The voices got closer, and Norman was trying to make out the words, when he froze. If he needed further proof that he was dead, he now had it. In front of him was the living reproduction of a page from his photo album: Aunts Elizabeth and Amy and baby Maria, age sixteen. The beautiful Gould sisters with their titian hair and saucer eyes, laughing gaily with a fourth beauty whose hair was as dark as theirs was light, whose eyes were as blue as the cornflowers he saw in one of the flowerbeds around the meadow. With them were three young men, only one of whom Norman recognized. It was Uncle Renzo, the uncle of less than a year, the uncle he never knew.

Amy and Elizabeth separated from the group and drifted toward the bush, but they couldn't see him. He wouldn't have cared anyway. He was so entranced by the blue-eyed girl. In all his life he'd never seen anybody so beautiful. And then—nothing.

He felt as though his head had been cracked open and realized he was lying on a hard surface. He moved his hands around him and raised his head. He was on the floor of the dining room, just outside the door to the back room. The cats in the kitchen had stopped yowling and the apartment was still. He rose from the floor and peered at the bed.

"Aunt Elizabeth . . . Aunt Amy?" he called softly. From the bundled furs he heard a faint snoring, as though his calling had set it in motion.

Now he walked over to the back room and pushed against the door. It was shut tightly, just as it had been during the afternoon. What had happened to him? It was obvious that he had passed out just before getting to this door. But that pain in his head. It felt as though somebody had hit him.

He staggered into the kitchen. The four cats sat together on the table and stared at him. They continued staring as he walked out the door.

5

He was about to hail a cab when he remembered he'd spent the last of his money on the turkey for Signe. Luckily, in his inside coat pocket, he found a subway token. The rattling of the train caused his head to throb and the pain got worse. I've never passed out in my life, he kept thinking, even amid all the shelling in Vietnam.

As soon as he got into his apartment he swallowed two

aspirins, musing that he should have kept some of the pain-killers he'd given to Aunt Elizabeth. Then he removed the stickpin from his pocket and examined it. Almost the size of a campaign button, it splashed its diamondlight at him and he wondered how much he could get for it, assuming he was prepared to live with the accompanying curse. Why had she laughed about it? Because, Norman, he told himself, you better face naked facts about your aunts—they're crazy or senile or both, and you shouldn't be surprised at anything they do or say.

He tossed the stickpin and the quarters into a cigarette box he kept on the coffee table, realizing those quarters would have paid for a taxi, if he'd remembered them. Then he removed all his clothes, dumped them into the hamper and showered.

He pulled his bed out of the couch and sat in it, thinking there must be something he should do now. "I know," he said to Fulcho, "I'll call Charlie and tell him." He walked into the little kitchen and took the telephone back into bed with him. It was six o'clock in Los Angeles. Charlie must be at the side of his pool.

"Dickens residence," said the velvet voice. "Mr. Dickens has a brother?" it added incredulously, then Charlie got on.

"Hey, Norman, baby," came the British-accented voice. "How've things been? Why don't I ever hear from you?"

"I think you're hearing from me now, Charlie."

"You're developing a sense of humor in your old age! I can't wait to tell Deirdre."

"Who's Deirdre?"

"Oh, don't you read *Women's Wear*? She's my new old lady. Justine and I split."

"I guess we're not the closest of families, Charlie," and he realized he hadn't talked to his only brother in months and hadn't seen him in four years. "Charlie—uh—I've been down to see Aunts Elizabeth and Amy."

"How are the old bags? Still alive?"

"Barely. Elizabeth seems very sick. I think she's dying.

Charlie, remember their apartment, how big it was? They gave up seven of the rooms and live in the three little rooms in the back with all the furniture and—"

Charlie was screaming with laughter.

"Charlie? Charlie, if you saw it you wouldn't think it was funny. It's stifling, and they don't seem to notice it. Do you . . . do you think we could get together some money to help them out?"

"Dear old Norman, let your big brother give you some sound advice. Good manners are one thing, but it's not necessary to be everybody's doormat. Let the old biddies go into a home. You're not responsible for them."

"I know that, Charlie." Charles the Beautiful, his mother used to call him. "I hope you grow up to be as wonderful as your older brother," she had always said. "A mother couldn't wish for a more perfect son." Perfect Charlie, the angel. If they ever made a movie of his life he would have to be played by Paul Newman, Robert Redford, Peter O'Toole and Jean-Claude Killy. "But, Charlie, I thought it might be a good idea to help them."

"Baby, I'm feeling the pinch. I still get my allowance. Justine's old man is afraid to lose face by cutting me off—besides I know where a few bodies are buried—but I've spent a fortune lately. Just got this new place in Benedict Canyon and that wasn't hot dogs. And the Rolls—you should see the Rolls!"

"What?"

"The Rolls, my new car."

"I thought you were talking about hot dog rolls."

Charlie laughed. "You're becoming an effing riot, kid brother. Do you know that?"

"Uh, yes, Charlie. How are the kids?"

"Daphne was into the drug scene, but she's clean now. I sent her to Hawaii for the holidays. Ronald is straight A and going to UCLA next semester. You know, I quit that rattrap."

"You're not teaching any more? What are you doing?"

"I thought you knew, Norm. Gave it up a year ago. It didn't

do a bloody thing for my creative juices. I'm working up properties now."

"What?"

"Motion picture properties. I've formed a production company.
We're going to be very hot. Say, when you coming out here?
We can put you up. Maybe I can make you into a movie star.
You still so good-looking?"

"I've covered all my mirrors so I won't be blinded. Charlie,
Aunt Elizabeth asked me tonight if you still have a lamp she
gave you—wisteria?"

"Are you serious? The Tiffany lamp? It's the centerpiece of
my house. I was offered sixteen thousand for it last week." He
chuckled. "I conned it out of the old girls right after Mom
died. I'm surprised they gave it to me. They were no dopes
when it came to antiques."

"Maybe they were just being generous."

"Hey, Norm, don't get maudlin on your old brother. Say, kid,
you need any clothes? I got eight suede jackets I never wear
any more."

"No, thanks. I just bought four new ones."

Charlie laughed again. "Hey, what's got into you, baby?"

"I'll call you again sometime, Charlie. Say hello to everybody."
He hung up.

"Fulcho, I just talked to my wonderful brother. I feel sorry
for everybody in the world, because they don't all have Charlie
for a brother. He should be bronzed."

It was because of Charlie the Splendid that Norman grew up
never feeling he had quite made it in anything. Charlie was the
first-born, and Norman arrived fourteen years later. "Not an
accident, really," his mother used to say with a laugh. "More
a love-child."

All through prep school and Princeton he'd been haunted by
the specter of Charlie. He remembered now rushing up to his
mother with an all A report card, at last matching the marks of
Charlie, and Maria had said, "It's very lovely, dear, but, you
know, A's were harder to get when Charlie was going to school."

Charlie could do nothing wrong. Charlie the Idealist, to whom money was meaningless, even though he had grown up with loads of it. And just to prove it he married one of the richest girls in California, and they lived on his teacher's pay, with a few extras thrown in by Justine's department-store-tycoon father —like a Beverly Hills mansion, a house at Malibu, several cars and unlimited access to dad-in-law's travel agent. The one positive thing Norman could say about his father was that he didn't like his oldest son; openly, in fact, called him a hypocrite. But Maria never saw through any of this, or, if she did, never acknowledged it.

Wonderful Charlie, who once invited Norman to vacation at his Malibu house and for the whole week treated him like a servant, because that was the way Charlie treated everybody. Marvelous Charlie, who was overheard to say during that same vacation, "Poor old Norman. I was brought up with money and class. All *he* got was the class." And dear Justine, always too good for Charlie, had quipped, "And most of the looks too, darling." Norman smiled, thinking about the expression on Charlie's face. That was the last time he'd seen him.

The pain in his head wouldn't go away. Nor would the memory of that beautiful blue-eyed girl. He thought about Linda and the dozens—was it hundreds?—of girls he'd known since Linda. All faceless. But he knew every line, every angle of that face in the garden.

By the time Fulcho strolled across his chest to lie under his arm Norman was fast asleep.

6

He raced up the subway stairs. It was nine forty-five. How could he have slept through the alarm? Even Fulcho had overslept. Sometime during this early morning he had lost count of the number of times he had been disturbed by dreams of that fantastically beautiful garden. He could almost still smell the flowers. More importantly, he could still see that unbelievable girl.

At the fourteenth floor he rushed through the crowd around the coffee wagon and fell into his chair without even removing his coat. It was nine forty-nine and he thought he would just sit there until he stopped huffing. He hadn't even noticed Mr. Perry standing outside his cubicle.

"Well," came the hated voice, and Norman narrowed his eyes, hoping to cut off the view of Perry's little face, with the bangs that covered the tops of his glasses. "I want to talk to you, Norman."

Norman stared at him, then remembered to remove his coat.

"I said I want to talk to you, Norman."

"Well, Mr. Perry, do you want to talk here or in your office?"

"Here will do." He folded his arms over his skinny oxford-gray chest. "I don't presume to know what you do in your off-hours, Norman, nor do I even want to hazard a guess, but I would like to remind you that starting time at the Donworth Company is nine fifteen A.M. What time is it now, Norman?"

Defeated, Norman looked at his watch. "Nine fifty-one."

"Yes, nine fifty-one, and do you know how many minutes you've stolen from the company so far?"

"Thirty-four."

"And how do you figure that? I get thirty-six!"

"I've been here for two minutes, Mr. Perry."

"Oh, well, aren't *you* the clever one. Now would you mind explaining your lateness?"

"I can't explain it, Mr. Perry. I guess I didn't hear my alarm. I was very tired. I went to see my aunt last night—"

"Oh, did you? I thought you were supposed to be ill yesterday."

"Well, I wasn't. I mean I was, but then I had to go out because my aunt is very sick—"

"You're sitting up with a sick aunt. How original."

"I wasn't trying to be funny, Mr. Perry."

"Your life is too complicated for me, Norman, but I'll deal with it on my own terms. You'll simply be docked for an hour for today and I expect that henceforth when you tend to your" —he raised his eyes skyward—"*sick aunt* you can manage to do it outside of company time."

Norman noticed a number of employees had gathered around his cubicle. And so, obviously, had Mr. Perry, because he now played to the crowd, one of his favorite activities. "I mean, Norman"—he chuckled—"you look anything but the type, but I'd hazard a guess that you were visiting your aunt in some motel." He smirked and swooped out.

Two members of the audience, Max O'Hara and Brad Horowitz, stayed on.

"Hey, old Norman," said Max, hitting him playfully on the knee. "You got yourself a little action going? You can tell us about it. We're your buddies. You're the only guy we know who never talks about his sex life. Maybe there's nothing to talk about, hah?" He and Brad began to laugh. "Maybe that's why Linda—"

Norman wheeled around so violently that he knocked his typewriter off the pull-out portion of his desk and it crashed to the floor. His fists were clenched, and Max and Brad's laughter was frozen. They stared at him, then walked out, laughing again.

"Well," he heard Max say, "this is the first time we ever got a rise out of him. Maybe he's joining the human race."

Norman lifted up the typewriter, put paper into it and tested it. It still worked. He heard the sound of a throat clearing and looked around. It was Sharon.

"Norman, I don't understand why you let them get away with that. And Mr. Perry. You should have reminded him about all the times you've stayed late or worked through your lunch hour. Hey, Norman, I'm going out on a limb again and even though you've given me an ingenious excuse every other time, I'm inviting you to dinner. How about it? I can make steak and spaghetti."

"That's very nice of you, Sharon, and I'm not making any phony excuses, but I really have to spend a lot of time with my aunt. She may be dying and they—She . . . there are two of them, and they expect me to go there, so I'd rather not make any plans I'll have to break."

Sharon shook her head and walked out.

Norman went to the reception room and asked Barbara, the receptionist, whether he could use the telephone. That, plus the noon to one P.M. lunch hour for all employees, plus a lot of other things, was one of the sick rules of the Donworth Company. Only executives—and on this floor that included Mr. Perry and two others—had telephones on their desks. Management felt it wasn't necessary to install instruments for any of the other employees, since it only encouraged personal phone calls. Emergency calls were allowed to come through at Barbara's desk.

He called the telephone company and after interminable waits, arguments and promises got their agreement to install a telephone at his aunts' apartment "as soon as humanly possible."

He turned to Barbara. "Would you do me a favor? Ask around if anybody wants to adopt a black female cat. I know one who needs a home."

"I'll put a note on the employees' bulletin board."

"Thanks."

Returning to the pile of letters on his desk, he flipped through them, noting four in Spanish, six in German, eighteen in Italian and fourteen in French. Forty-two letters he was expected to translate into English this morning, orders for merchandise from the Donworth Worldwide Mail Order Company. And after he forwarded the letters to the shipping department he would then have to complete a form note to the customer in his particular language, telling him either that the merchandise was enclosed, it wasn't in stock or the price had changed.

He picked up the first letter.

At lunchtime he shoved the undone letters under his desk blotter, put on his coat and rushed to the elevator, just missing the first wave of Donworth employees heading for the luncheonettes and sandwich shops in the neighborhood.

In fact he missed more than that. He missed the next hour and a half out of his life. When he looked at his watch again it was one thirty, he was seven blocks from the office and he hadn't remembered walking there. All that time had been spent wondering about that enchanted garden, wishing the dream had lasted long enough for him to have heard what they were saying.

Nobody noticed him going into his cubicle, so he assumed he was in the clear. He slipped the letters out from under his desk blotter and got to work. But every page he looked at reflected back a picture of the blue-eyed girl in his head.

He was on the last of the German letters, an order for matching red-white-and-blue hammocks, wondering what the writer's game was, when he felt a presence behind him and he started. It was Mr. Perry, all color drained from his face.

"Norman, you may think you're putting one over on the world, but I'd like you to know that *I* know what time you came back. Just what the hell do you think you're doing?"

I only wish I knew, Norman thought. "I'm sorry, Mr. Perry. I was wandering the streets. I guess I was so concerned about . . . my aunts that I lost track of the time."

"I'm not buying that story, Norman. I demand to know where you're going!" He was verging on hysteria and Norman thought, Who is this crazy person and why am I allowing him to get away with this?

He burst out with "Mr. Perry, I'll give you my aunts' address, if you want to check up on me. I'll even introduce you to them if you like. I'm not trying to rob the company of any time. I think you know I've always done a good job. But my aunt is very sick." The lilies-of-the-valley smell came back to him. He shook his head, as though it would dislodge the memory. "They're the only family I have left except for my brother in California, and I never see him at all."

Perry stared at him, then the huffiness vanished. The eyes softened and the little mouth relaxed. He smiled. "I never realized you could get so emotional, Norman. Maybe I've misjudged you. You know, I think you're in need of some vocational guidance. Why don't we meet after work? I'm sure we can straighten this out." He smiled as broadly as his mouth would allow, then wheeled around and zipped away.

Sharon came in and handed him a large batch of new letters. The top one was Italian, a good-luck sign, he thought.

"Norman, was Perry giving it to you for coming back late?" She was wearing a very light gardenia perfume, and Norman's gaze lingered longer on her chest than he'd intended.

"Yes, but he calmed down." He smiled. "Now he wants to be my friend and give me what he calls 'vocational guidance.'"

Her eyebrows lifted. "Really! When does he propose to do that?"

"He wants to see me after work."

She covered her mouth. "Are you going to see him?"

"I guess so."

"Norman, he doesn't want to talk about your career. In case you haven't noticed, you're extremely good-looking." She moved closer to him and touched his cheek. "Don't you know what he is, or don't you care?"

"Sharon, I may not be the fastest brain in town, but I'm a big boy." He smiled, feeling he had hurt her in some way. "I can take care of myself."

"I wonder," she said distractedly and drifted out. He stared after her, thinking she could have been one of the young Gould sisters—with the saucer eyes and the titian hair. And he wondered whether he was ever going to do anything about her.

By five ten, when a few score of Donworth's employees were on their mark for the five fifteen closing bell, Norman was just finishing the last of his afternoon correspondence, a handwritten letter from Bordeaux:

Dear Sirs:
  I am much interested in your gold-plated simulated jeweled heart with personal engraving, "To My One and Only Love." I would like to order six, in French, with one of the following names engraved on the back of each: Emma, Rosie, Molly, Lena, Minnie and Bessie. They are all to be signed: "Always, Oscar." Attached is check for proper amount, plus postage and addresses of each of the ladies.
                            Cordially,
                            Oscar Aixinburghe

Norman directed this one to Sharon's attention with his own note:

Dear Sharon,
  Please take care of enclosed. Do you have the nerve to send all of them to the wrong ladies?
                            Norman

By five fifteen the entire floor was empty and Norman cleared his desk. The smell of peppermint wafted at him and there stood Mr. Perry, reeking of instant mouthwash, in his natty salt-and-pepper tweed coat with velvet collar.

"Ready, Norman?" He looked odd and Norman realized this was the first time he'd ever seen him without his glasses. It seemed to change the shape of his nose and added age lines. Staring at the little leering mouth, Norman decided he wouldn't be able to face even half an hour alone with Perry.

"Uh, I was just about to head for your office, Mr. Perry. Something's come up. I won't be able to see you now. My aunt has taken a turn for the worse."

"But Norman, I've made reservations—"

"I'm sorry, sir, but I just can't."

Perry stared at Norman for several long moments. Then he nodded knowingly. "So that's the way it is, eh, Norman?" His face flushed and he looked as though he were going to scream. But, very quietly and very controlled, he said, "I won't forget this," and swooped out.

Norman put his coat on and left the deserted building. It was freezing out, but he decided he had to walk.

Drifting downtown past the antique shops and the Christmas tree sellers, the sounds of trucks grinding through his head, he wondered whether he would still have a job the next day.

He was shivering as he opened the door to Berkenblitt's Bargains.

Natalie, in a dark brown dress identical to yesterday's black one, gave him her malevolent smile. "Good evening," she said. "Did you give Mrs. Ferromonte my message?"

He nodded.

"I know she doesn't *like* to be called Mrs. Ferromonte, but that's my little joke. After all, she *was* divorced forty-four years ago or was it twenty-one years ago?" She gave him a sidelong glance and again he got that eerie frightened feeling.

"I don't know."

She touched his arm. He flinched and she smiled. "One of these days, perhaps you will. Things are quite different now than they used to be," she said as she assembled his order from her narrow shelves and cabinets. "Your aunts keep forgetting Simon Gould is dead and that they only had credibility in the milieu he created for them."

"Miss Berkenblitt, I don't know what you mean, but my aunt is sick and I wish you'd hurry."

She laughed that strange Hmm, hmm, hmm sound again and bagged the order. He opened the door so violently that the cowbells on back of it jingled noisily.

"Don't forget to tell them that Natalie was asking for them!" He shut the door on more laughter.

On the way up the stairs he wondered what this woman had against his aunts. That one day so many years ago when Elizabeth and Amy had invited her into their garden had obviously made a lasting impression on her. But what was that about forty-four years or twenty-one years?

Amy took a long time to open the door and then hobbled quickly away toward the dining room. The kitchen was dark.

"Aunt Amy," he said, pushing the wall switch, "why was the light off? Where are you going?" He put the package down and caught her by the arm as she went through the lace curtain separating the rooms.

"Let me go!" she whimpered. "I've got to go in there!"

"Why? Is something wrong with Aunt Elizabeth?" Amy stared at him, wild-eyed.

"What's the matter, Aunt Amy?" He went past her and turned the dining-room light on. The bed was the same litter of old furs, but Elizabeth wasn't there. "Where is she?" he asked.

Her eyes looked dreamy. In a singsong voice she said, "I don't know, I don't know. She must be someplace."

"Aunt Amy, where is she? In the hospital?"

Now Amy's eyes got shrewd. "I'm sure she'll be back quite soon. Just try to have a little patience."

"Aunt Amy, Aunt Amy." His hands were shaking. "Aunt Elizabeth can barely walk."

"Calm down, Norman. You always *were* a high-strung child. I know—let's play the movie game. T. H. A. H. N."

"I don't want to play the movie game, Aunt Amy."

She shook her head and began to cough.

Norman looked into the dining room again, and through the musty odor of the room he noticed a new smell, incense, just like last night. And music. He began to hear music again, coming from the back room. He stared at the door. That's where she was. He walked toward it.

Amy screamed, "No, don't! Don't go in there! Stay out, you willful child! You're not allowed!"

Then the door swung open and Aunt Elizabeth, surrounded by curls of smoke, almost fell against him.

"Norman, what the devil." She swung the door shut behind her, then began to breathe loudly through her mouth. "Norman, what are you doing here? I told you not to go near that room. It's dangerous for you. Why don't you ever listen to me, you foolish boy?" She was completely out of breath, and when she leaned on him he put his arm around her. She was so frail, he felt that if he pressed too hard he would break her in two. He lifted her up and carried her to the bed, then stood at its foot until her breathing sounded more normal.

"Aunt Elizabeth, if it's dangerous, why were you in there? Can't you get as hurt as I?"

Her eyes looked blank and she wheezed, "Nothing can hurt me when I'm there." She gasped and coughed and her tone changed. "Foolish, foolish child, you don't know where anything is in that room. I was just looking for my hot water bottle. I guess I must have given it away to somebody years ago." She raised her voice and added loudly, "Along with everything else I ever owned!"

"O.K., Aunt Elizabeth, I don't know what's going on around here," he said, his voice so angry he startled himself. "And I suppose it's none of my business, but you're the only family I have besides Charlie, and I want to help you. Why won't you answer my questions?"

Exasperatedly Elizabeth said, "What do you want to know, Norman?"

"First of all, why was incense burning in that back room? And where was the music coming from?"

Elizabeth sighed several times. "All right, Norman. I was in there and you *did* smell incense and you *did* hear music. I've developed a little habit in the last couple of years and I didn't know whether you'd entirely approve, especially since it's illegal. I was smoking grass."

"What!" Norman started to laugh uncontrollably. He had to hold on to the wall to steady himself. "Aunt Elizabeth, when did you start this?"

"Young man!" Elizabeth said sternly. "I'll have you know that at the age of seventeen I smoked an opium pipe! A very important Arabian sultan house-guested with us—remember Hakim, Amy?—and he turned me on to all the habits that your contemporaries think are their exclusive province. You might be additionally shocked to learn that there is almost nothing your generation has done that hasn't already been done by mine." Then she started to laugh. "Oh, Norman, if you could see the expression on your face."

"Oh, it's swell to have a good laugh now and again," Amy said. "It *was* all right to laugh, wasn't it, Elizabeth?"

Elizabeth's laughter changed to coughing and wheezing, then a combination of both. "Maybe it wasn't all right, Amy," she whispered, then doubled over, shaking.

"What is it?" Norman asked. "Can I get you some water?"

"No, darling, it's too late for water. Sometimes we're punished for our little excesses, aren't we? You know what I'd really like now, Norman? Some wine."

"Wine?"

"Yes, would you be a darling and get us some? Not expensive. I want it very sweet. Muscatel or malaga."

"I thought you had diabetes," he said.

"Well, that doesn't matter. Just get it. And— Come over here." She whispered the next. "When you return with the wine there's something very important I have to tell you."

"Why can't you tell me now?"

She shook her head impatiently. "The time isn't right. Take my word for that." He knew it was useless to pursue it.

On his way to the door he happened to glance over at the kitchen tables. "Aunt Amy, what became of the peonies?"

"The peonies?"

"Yes, the flowers I brought you yesterday. They're gone."

"Oh, I don't know. They must be around somewhere."

"We put them in a warmer place," Elizabeth called out. "That kitchen was far too cold for them."

As he'd done last night, Norman pushed the unlock button on the door.

He bought two bottles of muscatel and on the way back to the house tried to figure out why the Gould sisters, of the champagne palates, should want such stuff. No matter how poor they were, it just wasn't their style. Then he sighed, thinking he didn't really know what their style was any more.

He pushed open the door. Facing him, just as they had last night, were the four cats, sitting on the table meowing loudly.

"O.K., I'll feed you soon. Aunt Amy? Aunt Elizabeth?" No answer.

"Does anybody want some wine?" he called into the dining room, then pushed the curtain aside. The furs were lumped all over the bed and he started back into the kitchen again when he got a curious feeling about that bed and went back to check. There were just coats on it—no aunts. He switched the light on.

"Aunt Elizabeth? Aunt Amy?"

He tried to peer behind the piled-up furniture. They weren't —couldn't be—there. From the kitchen the cat yowling got louder and now he smelled that lilies-of-the-valley smell. He stared at the door to the back room. Well, they had to be in there. He pushed on the door and it swung open. He stepped away from it and looked around him. *This is exactly what happened last night. I imagined walking into that room and then— But I'm not imagining anything now. I'm here, standing up, and the door is open.*

"Aunt Elizabeth? Aunt Amy? Are you in here?" No sound. Just as he'd remembered from last night, there was that same twisting, tangled tree or bush. And again the smell of lilies got stronger. Just to make sure, he looked back. *Yes, I'm still standing. The dining room is out there and I'm in here and I'm still standing.* Now, as he remembered, he pushed his way through the tangle. Maybe they were hiding at the other end.

And he was there again. When he looked back, all he saw was the beautiful green bush through which he'd stumbled. It was as though he'd just stepped into a movie at the part at which he'd left it the day before. He was wearing the same beige silk suit. And the crowd of merrymakers were in the exact positions as in his vision of last night. He hid behind a statue and listened to their rapid Italian.

"I said I would not leave this country until I'd stamped on some grapes," said one of the girls. He thought it might be his mother.

"Stamped on grapes? We don't believe that story for a minute. Sounds like you have an assignation in the arbor." Was that Aunt Amy? he wondered.

Now they all laughed and Norman peered out and spotted the beautiful black-haired girl in the long white silk dress, a small pink flower pinned to its bosom. She seemed to maintain a kind of wistful reserve through the hilarity of the others. She stared at the statue, but she couldn't possibly be seeing him.

Well, he thought, go for broke. I might as well step out and introduce myself. If I'm dead it doesn't matter whether I'm trespassing.

He never got the chance.

"Elizabeth," one of the other girls called out, and Norman didn't know whether it was Amy or his mother, "I believe I see somebody hiding behind that statue there. Could it be Robertino?"

The group rushed toward the statue and Norman jumped up. They stared at him, fascinated.

"No," said Elizabeth, speaking rapid English now, "it isn't Robertino. It isn't anybody we know. Who are you, you most dazzling young man? Have you been sent by the God of Appia Antica? Larkey, is he a friend of yours?"

The lovely girl stared at him and said, in Italian, "I have only seen this man in my sleeping thoughts. I can't believe he is real."

"My God, Larkey," said Elizabeth in Italian, "that's almost depraved—though I can't say I blame you. Step over here to us, young man. We want you to introduce yourself."

Norman walked around the dahlia bed and came up to them. They continued staring at him soundlessly. "My name is Norman Dickens," he said in Italian.

"Dickens? That sounds English," said Amy.

"Bully for you, Amy!" Elizabeth laughed. "Are you related to Charles Dickens?"

"He's my brother," blurted Norman, and they all laughed.

"Dickens," said Uncle Renzo thoughtfully. "I have a young cousin named Dickens. He lives in Sicily. Are you from Sicily?"

"I'm from the United States," said Norman.

"Of course," said Aunt Elizabeth, smiling seductively. "They don't manufacture anything like you in Europe." Norman's attention was caught by the lovely Larkey. He smiled and her glorious eyes smiled back at him.

"Larkey," said Elizabeth, "if Monk—not to mention your parents—ever saw the way you're looking at Mr. Dickens, the entire engagement would be off."

"What engagement?" Norman asked Larkey.

She blushed.

"Larkey," said Uncle Renzo, "is engaged to Monk Abruzzi, one of the most powerful men in Rome."

If he weren't already dead, Norman would have wanted to die.

"One of the *richest* men in Rome, you mean," said Maria.

"I'll bet Daddy could match him—pound for lire!" said Amy.

"I'll bet nobody could match the two of you for crassness," Elizabeth said, and laughed. Very suddenly her laughter was choked off by the distant sounds of cats meowing. She stared at Amy, who took her arm and the two of them immediately walked away from the group and into the tangle of bushes through which Norman had come upon this fantastic scene. The meowing got louder, overwhelmingly louder, but none of the others seemed to hear it. It was so loud now that Norman covered his ears, but that didn't help. The meowing was going straight through his head.

He moved his lips, but no sound came out. Then, as though

by somebody else's power, he turned away from them and headed after Elizabeth and Amy, through the thorny bushes, through the pitch blackness. It was only his constant movement that kept the wild meowing under control. He pushed his way through the branches and then . . . and then . . .

7

"Norman, Norman, get up." His head was aching, and surrounding him were the crowded chairs and tables of Elizabeth and Amy's apartment.

"Amy, dear, hurry. Get some water to sprinkle on him. Oh, poor dear Norman!"

Norman opened his eyes. He was lying on the floor of the dining room. "What happened?" he asked.

"Don't you know?" Elizabeth asked sternly.

"Yes. Those cats began to meow and then you and Amy left the garden and I followed you."

"Hurry, Amy, he's delirious."

"Last night I thought it was a dream. I thought we were all dead. But now I know. How did we get there?" A great volume of water splashed over his face and he jumped up.

"Amy," shouted Elizabeth. "I didn't say drown him. Norman, darling, you shouldn't get up so quickly. You've had a bad knock. I warned you not to go into that room. Only Amy and I can find our way about in there. It's a miracle you weren't killed, with a candlestick falling on your head that way."

"What candlestick?" he asked.

"Why, one of our large candelabra fell on you, dear. We were so afraid you might have been seriously hurt."

"Aunt Elizabeth, the same thing happened last night. You can't tell me I was knocked on the head."

"Well, what can I tell you, Norman? Do you wish me to make up a fairy story? And what is this about last night? You weren't hit by a candlestick last night."

"No, but I was hit by something."

"Norman, explain yourself. You paid us two lovely visits and then you went home. At no time were you knocked unconscious."

Norman sighed. "I came back here last night after you were both asleep." He stared at the bundles of coats all over the bed. They had looked the same way with his aunts under them. Had they really been in that bed last night before he went into that room?

"Aunt Elizabeth, listen to me, please. I saw you and Aunt Amy and my mother and Uncle Renzo in the beautiful garden and everybody was talking in Italian."

"You saw nothing, child," Elizabeth said gently. "You saw something from out of a dream. You saw something from my dreams. Would your Aunt Elizabeth ever lie to you, the most precious child in the whole world?"

"Aunt Amy, when you were young, did you ever know a girl named Larkey?"

"Larkey, certainly. Such a pretty little thing. She was engaged to marry Monk Abruzzi."

"That's more than enough, young lady," Elizabeth said sternly. "Yes, Norman, we knew a girl named Larkey. Why?"

"Well, I saw her. I just saw her with you in that garden."

"Do you hear the child, Amy? Oh, my feet pain me so. Norman, you didn't see Larkey, you didn't see anybody. You went into that room where you had no business going, and you got hit on the head. And if I didn't love you so much I'd say you had it coming to you for disobeying me."

"O.K., I was hit on the head, Aunt Elizabeth. How would you explain my knowing Larkey?"

"How would I know? I imagine your mother used to talk about her a lot. She was a dear friend of ours during our Italian period."

"My mother never mentioned her name to me."

"Perhaps you saw her picture in an album."

"We have an album full of pictures and none of Larkey. And even if there was, color film hadn't been invented in the 1920s. How would I know she had blue eyes?"

"She had the bluest eyes." Amy sighed.

"Amy," Elizabeth warned, "you must not encourage him in this lunacy."

"I wasn't encouraging him," Amy singsonged. "A fact is a fact, Lizbeth. Larkey had blue eyes."

"Just a minute, Aunt Elizabeth. One more question and that'll be the end. Where were you when I came back to the apartment with the wine?"

"Norman, dear," Elizabeth said, "I have a confession that shouldn't surprise you. Your wicked aunts were both in that back room." She and Amy began to laugh.

I'm really going mad, he told himself.

"Well, now you know," said Elizabeth.

"Know what?" Norman demanded.

"We were, oh, we were turning on, silly boy." Then she looked at Amy. "Turning on together is the rule, Amy. We must not turn on one another."

"Aunt Elizabeth," he said very quietly, "why didn't I see you when I went in there?"

"Oh," Amy said, covering her mouth.

"I told you, darling," Elizabeth said, smiling, and ran her hand over his hair. "You don't know the room as well as we do. We saw you and we called out, and the next thing you know the candlestick fell on you."

"I didn't smell marijuana. I smelled lilies of the valley."

"Well, that's the new paper we're using. Now, Norman, be a good boy, and don't try your Auntie Elizabeth any more. Lord knows, it's a wonder I didn't have a heart attack when you were knocked out. Oh, Amy, I'm so weak. Help me to bed."

"I'm sorry, Aunt Elizabeth," Norman said as he helped her to lie down.

"No sorrier than I. You've had a bad time of it, but I'll make it up to you. I'm going to give you ten dollars for your trouble coming down here. How does that suit you, child?"

"You don't have to give me any money."

"Oh, you're not getting out of here so easily. Amy, get the Baccarat heart. Hurry."

"Forget it, Aunt Elizabeth," Norman said. "Save the money for your old age."

She laughed. "My old age. Oh, Norman. Well, when shall we have the pleasure of seeing you again?"

"Maybe tomorrow."

"Come over here. I want to kiss the dimple on that sweet chin of yours." He walked over and she threw her arms around him. "Oh, Norman, darling, you're all we have. We love you so and we're so sorry."

"Sorry? For what?"

"That we can't entertain you properly here. That we can't offer you a meal, a chance to sup with us."

"That's all right, Aunt Elizabeth." His head felt as though it was being sandpapered. "I guess I'd better go." He walked toward the kitchen then remembered something. "What was the important thing you were going to tell me tonight?"

"What?"

"You said you were going to tell me something important, remember?"

"I forget," she said imperiously.

In the kitchen Amy stood at attention, holding out the can opener as though it were a rifle at present-arms. The four cats stood around her feet, staring up at him. He opened the cat food and put it in front of them.

"Don't forget to feed Signe," Amy said. "She's been quiet as a mouse all day. Hasn't raised a yowl or anything. I've never known her to be so peaceful."

Norman smiled. "Probably overstuffed."

"Overstuffed?" Amy said. "She hasn't eaten all day."

"Well," he said, "she ate so much last night I think she must have filled up for the week."

"When did you feed her last night?" Amy asked.

"Oh," Norman said, "on the way here last night I decided to give the poor thing a break and I bought her some turkey."

"Oh, my God, oh, my God," wailed Elizabeth from inside.

"What's the matter?" shouted Norman.

"You'd never understand," Elizabeth said, her voice commanding again. "Here we've been on the verge of starvation and you fed turkey—turkey!—to that thing in there!"

"Well, so what? It isn't as though I was feeding blood to a vampire."

Amy hobbled over to the pantry and opened the screen door.

"Here, Signe, darling, here Signe," she called, then switched on the light. "Elizabeth, she's gone."

"Oh, God," moaned Elizabeth.

Norman looked over Amy's shoulder at the empty pantry.

"Why did you let her loose?" Amy accused.

"I didn't. I know I closed the door behind me after I fed her."

"Oh, Norman, what have you done? To your own flesh and blood," Elizabeth cried.

"Come on," he said, "don't get hysterical. She must have pushed the door open and was so happy to have a little freedom that she's hiding under something. I'll find her."

"Oh, Norman, you let her loose. Now we're finished."

"Aunt Amy, you're overstating the case. O.K., she fights with the other cats. You're acting as though she's a monster. I'll find her before I go and put her back."

"No, you won't," Elizabeth shouted.

"Don't worry, Aunt Elizabeth, she's got to be somewhere."

Elizabeth's voice was cool again, and at its most commanding, and as soon as she began talking, Amy's wailing stopped.

"Norman, darling," she said, "this absurd little incident has got us all a bit overheated. Please forgive us our excesses. We're two old ladies and—you're right—we're overstating the case. You go home, darling. You've been through enough tonight, and Amy will find Signe and return her to the pantry. Just get a good night's sleep."

He looked toward the back room. "Aunt Elizabeth, I'll be glad to stay and look."

She ignored him completely and sang out, "Oh, Amy, love, you have two minutes to give me the names of all four Marx Brothers."

"Oh, that's too easy." Amy laughed. "Groucho, Harpo, Chico and . . . and . . ."

"Too easy, is it? A minute and a half."

"Groucho, Harpo, Chico and . . ."

"Zeppo," said Norman quietly.

"Oh, you," Amy said. "I would have gotten it eventually."

Norman closed his eyes, then blinked them open again. He said good night quickly and left.

He wandered streets, not feeling the cold, wondering whether he had really lost his mind. How could a cat escape from a locked pantry? Why had Elizabeth switched gears so suddenly and told him not to bother looking for Signe? Was he just about to discover something they didn't want him to discover? Or was it just because a sliver of reason still existed in those muddled heads and they realized they were making too much of it? And, most important, had he really been hit on the head by a candlestick? No, the alternative was too preposterous. It was some kind of dream, a continuing dream. But why did he have this feeling that his heart was going to leap from his chest to go look for Larkey? He realized now, finally, that he had never really loved Linda, had never loved anybody before.

He was so preoccupied that he collided with the Christmas tree in his lobby, knocking off and smashing several of its decorations, including the large gold star of Bethlehem at the top. When he bent to pick up the pieces, the elevator operator rushed over and said, "Don't bother, Mr. Dickens. It could happen to anybody after a few Yuletide spirits, right? I'll clean it up."

When he reached his apartment the telephone was ringing. It was Sharon.

"Norman, I'd be the last person on earth to push myself on someone, but I called because I was concerned. How'd you make out with Perry?"

"The important thing is Perry didn't make out with me. I stood him up."

"Norman, is this you talking? I can't believe it. Are you all right?"

"I guess so. I have a headache. I got hit on the head."

"Oh, my God!"

"I wasn't mugged. Something fell on my head at my aunts' house."

"Now you listen to me, Norman. I happen to be at Lincoln Center, which, my street map tells me, is around the corner from you, and if you won't call me a brazen hussy I'd like to come over. Do you have any food in the house?"

"I guess."

"O.K., I'm coming over and cook you dinner."

"That would be very nice, Sharon."

"Well, he actually said yes to something. We may even start a relationship."

Sharon arrived with red wine and made omelettes and strong coffee. And because he was in a state of yearning, and because she was there and smelled nice, he started a relationship with her.

Sharon's kiss collided with Larkey's and he knew he was in the real world because Fulcho's hot body was asleep on his left arm.

"What time is it?" he asked.

"That certainly is terrific love talk, Norman. Is that all you can think of to ask?"

"Sorry. I'm just finding out where I am."

"I'm sorry, too. That was a bitchy thing to say, especially after you were so nice to me before."

"I try my best," he said.

"And you sure succeed—for a man of mystery, that is. Nobody really knows you, Norman. Why did it take so long to finally say yes to a date with me?"

"If I'm a mystery to you, think of how much more mysterious I must be to myself." He laughed.

"That lady did quite a hatchet job on you, didn't she?"

"I didn't know you knew Linda. She left the company years before you got there."

She began to write her name on his chest with her fingernail. "Norman, in an automobile accident, you don't have to examine the car to know what's wrong with the victim. Why are you laughing? It wasn't that funny."

"I'm ticklish. See, now you know one more thing about me."

"She must have been crazy to give you up."

"That feels nice," he said.

"I kind of thought you'd think that."

He put his arms around her and Fulcho was very grumpy about losing his warm spot.

"God Rest Ye Merry Gentlemen" was blaring in his ear from his clock radio, the time was seven-thirty and there was a note propped against the lamp.

Dear H. H.:

A respectable girl can't come to work two days in a row in the same outfit. You know how people talk. So I've gone home. I washed out the coffee pot and it's all ready with new coffee in it. Just light the stove. When we next meet I would like you to explain the following: (1) Why does a recluse keep three bottles of champagne chilling in his refrigerator? (2)

What is that sparkling "thing" in the cigarette box on this table? I didn't mean to pry, was just looking for a cigarette. I assume it's not diamonds. If it is, you really must be Prince Norman. (3) Why is your cat named Fulcho? (4) Why does that same cat hate me?

Your new friend.

His headache was gone and he knew the day had a chance if he could only force himself to stop thinking about Larkey and that ridiculous back room.

He was at his desk at eight forty-five. In his In box were forty-two orders, all in Italian. He flipped through the letters, then tossed them aside. Stop looking for a message from a girl who doesn't exist, he told himself.

A scent of cool air and light perfume behind him warned him about a girl who did. Again he was amazed at how much Sharon looked like the Gould sisters.

He pulled her to him and kissed her lightly on the cheek.

"Excuse me," said a prissy voice behind her as the bangs of Elliott Perry came into view. "Good morning, Miss Reynolds. I wonder whether you'd excuse Norman and myself for a few minutes?"

"Sure," she said flippantly, then to Norman, "Talk to you later. I want to discuss that romantic Frenchman's order for those monogrammed hearts." And she flounced out.

Perry, still wearing his coat, stared at Norman for a long time. Oddly enough, Norman didn't feel obligated to break the silence. He just stared back expectantly.

Perry cleared his throat, then shook his head. "Norman, I hardly know what to say to you today. I was willing to give of my time to help you." He switched from world-weariness to anger. "And don't think I haven't better things to do with my time than devote it to what's laughingly known as your career. Well, aren't you going to say something?"

"I don't know what to say, Mr. Perry."

"That's your whole trouble, Norman. You never know what to

say." Norman felt Perry's eyes assessing him. "Well, I'm just giving you fair warning. You're not getting away with any more around here and that's final." He marched away, almost colliding with the receptionist.

"Norman," she said, "you have a phone call."

At Barbara's desk Norman was told by the telephone company representative that his emergency request for a telephone for the Misses Gould was being filled that afternoon, "sometime between two and six P.M.," and would there be somebody there to receive the installation man? No, they couldn't pinpoint the time any more specifically.

This meant that Norman would have to leave the office at lunchtime and maybe not come back at all. He returned to his desk and tried to figure out the best way to approach Perry, then distracted himself by doing some of his letters. At eleven he strode to Perry's office, determined to ask him straight out.

"Mr. Perry is at an executive board meeting that's going to continue through lunch," his secretary snapped. Miss Prentiss had orange hair and a perennially disdainful expression and always reminded Norman of a dried apricot—except that dried apricots tasted good.

"I can't interrupt the meeting, no matter how urgent the request," she said. "You'll just have to work your problems out on your own." She turned away and continued her crossword puzzle.

When the noon lunch crush began, Norman wrote Mr. Perry a note:

Dear Mr. Perry:

The telephone company is installing an emergency phone in my aunts' apartment today between two and six. Since you weren't around to give me permission, I had to leave. If the man installs the phone early I will be back as fast as possible. If not, please have the accountant deduct the time from my pay. I promise this will not happen again.

Sincerely,
Norman Dickens

"Norman, dear, we weren't expecting you so early," Amy said as she opened the door.

"Did you find the cat?"

"Cat?" she asked blankly.

"Yes, Signe. Did you find her?"

"What?"

Was it possible he hadn't asked the question correctly?

"Signe. The cat who escaped from the pantry."

"Oh, not yet. She'll come out when she's hungry enough." She laughed, then began flicking the feather duster around. "How is it you're so early today?"

"I called the telephone company and they're putting a phone in here this afternoon."

"I don't want a phone," called Elizabeth from the dining room. "I've lived these eight years without one and I don't want a telephone bringing me bad news."

"Listen to me, Aunt Elizabeth," said Norman. "You can have your own way about anything you like, but it's dangerous for the two of you to be here alone and out of touch with me."

"We can get Pearlie Gish upstairs to call if we need you," implored Amy.

"I won't let them in!" shouted Elizabeth.

"O.K., Aunt Elizabeth, then I think you should know something." *Think of something, Norman, think of a big enough lie.* "I wasn't going to tell you this, but I got a call yesterday from this building's manager. He threatened to dispossess you in thirty days unless I could promise there would be somebody responsible caring for you, making sure this apartment doesn't burn down or that the cats don't overrun the house. Incidentally, he says cats aren't allowed in the building, but he agreed to look the other way if I promised to take charge. And he insisted the best proof I could offer was if I established telephone contact with you. It's the only way you can stay in this apartment."

"Oh, dear, oh, dear," Elizabeth said, then paused. "Why should the building manager be concerned about who cares for us? What business is it of his?"

"Managing the building is his business, Aunt Elizabeth. Now,

I can cancel the telephone and try to help you find a new apartment—"

"No, let the man come. Oh, why did this have to happen to us?" She was quiet for a while, then the command returned to her voice. "In what room is he going to put the phone?"

"Wherever it's most convenient," Norman said. "Wasn't there once a telephone in there?" He pointed toward the back room.

"Yes, there was, but it's not there now. I want the phone in the kitchen, Norman. Is that clear?"

Victory. "Certainly, Aunt Elizabeth. And I tell you what, I'll pay the bill for the first year. That'll be my Christmas present to you."

"No it won't. We can still afford to pay our own way."

"Can't I give you a Christmas present, Aunt Elizabeth? You've been giving me presents all my life."

"Why, Norman, darling, how touching. But no. We'll pay for it. I'll let you know another day what we want for Christmas."

Norman was silent. Then after a while Elizabeth said, "How can we let the man in here the way the place looks? Amy, you'll have to neaten up."

"Neaten up, Aunt Elizabeth? Do you have some dynamite?"

"Aunt Amy," Norman said after they stopped laughing, "I'm going to move some of the furniture out of here to make room for the installer."

"Where do you plan to put it?" Elizabeth asked.

"In the bathroom, I guess."

And for the next hour and a half Norman moved chairs, umbrella stands and whatever other bric-a-brac he could transport into the bathroom. When he finished, it resembled the other rooms.

He looked around the kitchen. Well, he thought, this is as good as it's ever going to be. The room still had a musty smell. "I'm going out to get some room spray. Is there another grocery nearby besides Natalie's?"

"Why?" Amy asked.

"Because I don't like to go in there."

"You have to go there," Elizabeth called. "I don't want her to think— Norman, darling, do you know the expression 'noblesse oblige'? Just because she is a vile creature is no reason to turn our backs on her."

"O.K. Aunt Amy, please give me the key."

Amy reached into the pocket of her kimono and handed him a key attached to a blue diaper pin, and he wondered whether it had once been his.

"What do you need the key for?" Elizabeth asked.

"So Aunt Amy won't have to rush to the door when I come back."

His first stop was a locksmith on Fourth Avenue, where he had a duplicate key made for himself. Then he walked back to Berkenblitt's Bargains.

The witch was clad in black again.

"Good afternoon, Norman. Have they found the cat yet?"

He looked at her blankly.

She flared her nostrils and said in a soft, menacing voice, "I asked you a question, Norman. Did Signe turn up?"

"Not yet." How did she know Signe was gone? Needless to ask. Somebody had told somebody had told somebody in this endless network of eccentric ladies.

"I shouldn't be surprised if she were gone for good." She raised an eyebrow." "I gave her to them, you know."

Norman forced a smile. "That was very nice of you."

"Well, I certainly thought so. But some acts of generosity are never appreciated," she said, smiling.

He left the store, trying to erase that smile from his eyes.

When he opened the door, Amy was standing in the doorway between the dining room and kitchen, the lace curtain hanging over her like a mantilla.

"You're making this place into a proper doll's house," she said.

Norman stared at her. "Yes, Aunt Amy, and as soon as the telephone is connected, I'm calling *Better Homes and Gardens* to send a photographer."

While they were still laughing, the bell rang from downstairs and Amy leaped into the dining room. "I must change into something appropriate," she said.

Norman opened the door and waited in the hallway. A very young telephone installer plodded up the stairs, then stood in the doorway. He seemed completely unfazed by the chaotic furniture arrangement. Thank God for the new life styles, thought Norman, indicating where he wanted the phone placed. Within forty minutes the telephone was connected and the wonderful sound of the dial tone echoed in Norman's ear.

"You can come out now, Aunt Amy," he called. "You can even call somebody if you like."

"I have nobody to call," she said plaintively as she hobbled into the kitchen.

"That phone will never be used," Elizabeth muttered.

"Well," Norman said, "I guess I'd better get that furniture out of the bathroom. Aunt Elizabeth, why don't I store some of it in your back room?"

"Why are you forever harping on that back room?" Elizabeth cried. "Are you looking for another accident? Why can't you stop torturing me?"

Why am I putting up with this? he wondered. Why don't I just walk out the door and never come back? Because I love these two old women, because I'm all they have. And if I walk out now I'll never know any more about Larkey.

He pulled his coat off one of the umbrella stands. "O.K., Aunt Elizabeth. I won't bring it up any more."

"When will we see you again?" asked Amy.

"I don't know," Norman said stiffly. "Aunt Elizabeth wants me to stop torturing her, so it might be better if I don't come around here for a while."

"No, no, you can't do that," said Amy, hobbling to the dining-room doorway. "You listen to me now, Elizabeth. You're not going to drive Norman away like everybody else! You'd better apologize."

"Apologize yourself. That's your specialty."

Amy let out a wail and threw herself on Norman, sobbing against his coat. "Oh, God help me. She took everything away from me my whole life long." She turned away and limped quickly back to the dining room. "You never let me get married," she cried. "You wouldn't let me out of your sight! At least you had a husband."

"Not quite," Elizabeth said dryly.

Amy turned to Norman. "Elizabeth's little lamb—that's what they used to call me."

"Uh, Aunt Amy," he said, "I really have to go."

"Wait, Norman, wait!" she screamed. Then: "Elizabeth, please, tell Norman you're sorry—even if you don't mean it." Her sobs almost muffled what she said next. "I think you've said enough. Please, I promise to behave."

Elizabeth, in a conciliatory tone, called, "Norman, darling, come here to me."

He walked over to the bed.

"You mustn't always take everything I say seriously, precious." She chuckled. "It's the pain that's talking. Sometimes I don't even know what I'm saying. Norman, I don't want you to go. Without you we'd die. Now, come on, stay for a snack with us. It'll be like the good old days when you were a roly-poly little boy."

"Not tonight, Aunt Elizabeth," he said, running his hand over his forehead. "I have a headache and I want to—" He looked at his watch. It was five ten. The office was closing. "I just want to go home and rest."

"Better not neglect your health, young man. Look at the two glaring examples around you." She laughed.

He headed for the door. "I'll call you tomorrow. Isn't it nice you have a telephone now?

"Norman, don't give the number out to anyone!"

He laughed. "Who might be asking for it?"

"You never know," she said meaningfully.

He swung the door open and almost collided with a dwarf-like woman in her sixties or seventies, wearing a white teddy-bear coat and a red and green stocking cap, with a pair of red-rimmed eyeglasses. He gasped.

She smiled at him, then looked into the apartment.

"Pearlie," said Amy, "this is my wonderful nephew, Norman. Isn't he handsome? Norman, this is my neighbor, Pearlie Gish, who called you the other night and is always so nice to us. Come in, Pearlie."

"I'm pleased to make your acquaintance," she said to Norman, and then motioned with her chin toward the dining room and asked Amy, "How is she?"

Amy shook her head. "As ever."

Norman said goodbye and was about to walk down the stairs when he heard Pearlie saying, "Some good-looking boy. What's he do for a living?"

"I don't know," said Amy. "We've been trying to figure it out. Says he works for an export company as a translator. It sounds suspicious."

"How does he manage to get the time off to visit you?"

"That's another thing. Elizabeth put two and two together and thinks the whole business about languages and exports— and, you know, his father originally came from Sicily—she thinks Norman works for the Mafia."

"The Mafia!" shrieked Pearlie, and Norman was grateful for the shriek, because he couldn't control his wild laughter. He ran down the stairs and laughed all the way to the corner.

9

As he approached Gramercy Park, Norman decided to return and listen at the door one more time in case . . . in case . . .

Pearlie was just leaving as he hit the landing below the apartment.

"Listen, honey," she said to Amy, "if you need anything, give me a call. Now that you have a phone we can talk like two hens."

His aunts were lucky, he thought, to have that little crone for a friend. Every now and then, despite his disillusionment with everybody, he was still surprised by somebody's kindness or gentleness. What did Pearlie have to gain by helping Elizabeth and Amy? Nothing. She was just being nice, because she was nice.

Outside the door, he heard the rustling made by the cats and some scattered conversation. Fourteen minutes after he had begun listening he heard strains of *Aïda,* and no further talk from either of the women. Using his key, he quietly opened the door. Amy was not in the kitchen. The four cats sat on the table eying him silently.

"Aunt Amy? Aunt Elizabeth?" He tiptoed into the dining room. The light was on and they weren't there. He stared at the sealed back-room door. All right, Norman, he said to himself, they're either in there smoking or . . . I'll find out. He swung the door open and the sweet smell of mint assailed him.

"Aunt Elizabeth? Are you in here? It's Norman. I came back to see . . . whether you were all right." Silence.

As he'd done before, he pushed his way through the labyrinthine branches and then—he was there again. It was dusk and he heard the lonesome calls of a bird and then the sound of Elizabeth, Amy and Maria on a nearby swing, being pushed by Renzo, who was singing loudly from *Aïda*. A bucket of champagne was on the grass and a servant was filling glasses.

"Oh, Lord," said Maria in English, "when I die I want my will to stipulate that champagne is to be poured over my grave every day."

Amy asked, "What sort of flowers would live through that?"

"Who needs flowers over a grave?" Maria answered. "Why not just grow grapes?"

"Listen to her at sixteen," Amy laughed. "Can you imagine what she will be by twenty?"

"Assuming we allow her to reach twenty," Elizabeth said, and Norman realized what he'd never noticed before: his mother and her sisters had identical voices, varied only by the dictates of their personalities. Maria's was a lazy, slightly mocking drawl. Amy's had a naïve enthusiasm. And Elizabeth's riveted your attention, like the flick of a finger against crystal.

He looked around for Larkey but couldn't see her, then moved to hide behind the same statue as he had the last time. He almost stepped on her, sitting on the ground, twirling a glass of champagne in her hands.

She smiled at him. "I knew if I waited here you would come again," she said. The flimsy garden dress was the color of her eyes, trimmed with tiny hand-painted buttons, each depicting a different flower. A pink peony bud rested in her bosom. The bottom curl of her hair brushed across the peony as she talked.

"Funny," he said in Italian, "because I thought I would never see you again."

"But I knew you would."

"How could you? I'm from another world."

"All people are from other worlds. What's important is that we are now in the same one."

He sat down beside her and noticed he was wearing a velvet suit the same color as Larkey's dress.

"But I'm really from another world—from a time ahead of this. I'm from 1973."

She laughed. "You are so admirable in 1928, I cannot wait to meet you in 1973."

"You never will. Elizabeth and Amy won't let me."

"You need not worry about them. I am independent of anybody."

"Except Monk Abruzzi," he said, and she looked away from him and stared down at the grass. He took her hand. "Are you in love with him?"

She tore some grass from the ground and tried to knot the blades together and he took them from her.

"What does it matter?" she asked in a tiny voice. "I am soon to be married to him."

He took both her hands and lifted her face so their eyes were level. "You don't have to marry him. You don't have to marry anybody."

"But I do," she said. "My parents have made all the arrangements."

"Can't you tell your parents to call it off?"

"What?" she asked, and he realized he had answered her in English. He asked her again in Italian.

"This is not the sort of marriage one calls off," she said, shaking her head. Then she removed one of her hands from his grasp and traced the outline of his chin. "This marriage has been arranged to please my parents and to allow them to be financially secure for the rest of their lives. I too will be financially secure, and I shall make Monk a good wife. He is not, after all, such a bad sort."

"Nobody has to do that any more," he said. "You sound like something out of an old story." Then he reminded himself he was forty-five years back in time.

She smiled. "You have obviously never been poor, because if you were you would know what it is like."

Even in this world they thought he was rich.

"I can't believe you," he said. "You look like a princess."

She laughed. "I am a princess. That's the sad part of my

story." She took his hand. "You see, my mother was very young and beautiful when she worked in the household of Prince Francesco Barberini Fabbro. And the prince dazzled her with his title and his charm and his good looks. Soon my mother was pregnant and was shipped away by the prince's family. I was born to her in Naples when she was eighteen. Prince Fabbro, my father, saw to it she had a tiny monthly allowance, just enough to feed and clothe their daughter, but she had to go to work right after I was born and she has never stopped working. Even the amount of money my stepfather earns has never been enough to keep the family going. My stepfather married my mother when I was four years old and he has been the only father I have ever known. My mother told him my father was a soldier named Barberini and, thus, my last name. But I am really the Princess Barberini Fabbro. Nobody knows it but my mother and the prince, and now you. The only inheritance I ever had from him was my small talent."

Norman stared at her, and she pointed to the little flowered buttons on her dress. "My father, the prince, is a very talented artist. I paint tiny little things, buttons and pins and miniature portraits. My mother says my painting is something like his, but nobody would ever make the connection. I have told you all this because I want you to know everything about me."

He leaned over and kissed her and now he knew why all the poetry in the world had been written.

"Oh, Norman Dickens," she said, beginning to cry. "Why did we not meet in another life?"

But we did, Larkey. "We can change all this. Can I talk to your mother?"

"When Mindelena Paoli makes up her mind to something there is no talking to her. Besides, the arrangement is made with Monk and he would not permit any alteration. He is not only the richest and most powerful man in Rome, but he can also be the most vengeful. I do not think you have enough evil in you to combat him."

"Do you have to have evil to combat evil?" he asked, and laughed. "How old are you, Larkey?"

"Nineteen. How old are you?"

He blinked. "I'm . . ." This is 1928, he thought, nineteen years before I'm born. "I'm also nineteen," he said. "Minus nineteen."

"Minus nineteen? I do not understand your American ways. But you look more mature." She laughed. "Shall we walk?"

"Sure," he said, "but I'd rather not be seen by Elizabeth and Amy."

She looked at him curiously, then shrugged. "I know a way. Follow me. We can hop from statue to statue until we come to the entrance."

They played this little game and very quickly were out on a narrow old road bounded by ancient walls, with little flowers growing through the cracks in the polished cobbles.

"What is this road called?" he asked.

She laughed. "Well, Norman Dickens, since you persist in playing this other-world game, I will let you guess."

"I know we're in Italy, because that was Uncle Lorenzo."

"Uncle Lorenzo?" She laughed.

"Oh, that was just a joke. And I know he lived somewhere outside Rome. So this must be—I don't know what it is,"

She laughed again. "Via Appia Antica."

"The Old Appian Way," he said in English.

"Why do you translate?"

"I don't know. It's a funny habit I got into."

They walked silently, holding hands, for a long distance, passing bits of ancient statues along the way, until they came to a curved brick building whose top looked like the crown of a king on a deck of cards. She led him through the gate.

"What is this?" he asked.

"It is the tomb of Cecelia Metella. I come here often."

They went inside and walked around, touching the stone engravings, vases, the remains of ancient sculpture. Girls and young men, arm in arm, strolled around, chattering, laughing.

"Why do you come here often?" he asked.

"You do not like it?"

"Yes, I do, but I just wanted to know why you come here."

"Because it reminds me that my troubles are not so large. When I see the work of thousands of years preserved here I know that I am really meaningless."

He put his arm around her waist. "You are not meaningless, Larkey. Not to me."

She put her hand over his mouth. "Let us go. I just saw a friend of Monk's and I do not want him to tell Monk he saw me here."

They walked back without speaking. The garden was empty.

"Where is everybody?" he asked.

"They must have gone back into the house. I am very late. Monk has probably arrived and everybody is all dressed and I have still to dress for dinner. Oh, Norman, I must go, and so must you." She threw her arms around him and kissed him and then started to run away.

He followed and caught her arm. "Larkey, when will I see you again?"

She looked around, troubled. "I don't know. Perhaps tomorrow night. Monk has business to transact in Rome and he will not come calling at all. Or perhaps it is better that we do not see each other any more."

"Do you want me not to come?"

"Oh, Norman, what a question to ask."

"Then I'll see you tomorrow night." He grabbed her arms and kissed her, and she started away again.

"Larkey!" he called.

She turned around.

"I love you."

She nodded, turned away and ran toward the house.

Norman reluctantly walked to the cluster of bushes and made his way through. The dusty smell told him he was back. But where were Elizabeth and Amy? He knew he was in the back room, but it was locked. He hammered on the door. "Aunt Elizabeth, Aunt Amy, it's Norman. Let me out!"

"Norman?" he heard Amy mutter. "Norman?"

"What the devil," Elizabeth said.

The door was opened by Amy, and he stepped out to see Elizabeth staring at him coldly.

"Well," she said, "I hope you've learned your lesson, Norman."

"Lesson?" he asked.

"Yes. If Amy hadn't talked me out of it I would have kept you locked in there all night."

"What are you talking about?" Amy asked her sister.

"Shut your beastly little mouth!" Then she turned to Norman and assumed a sweet tone. "Norman, we saw you go in. We were in the back room, and we decided not to let you know we were there. Then we sneaked out and locked the door just to teach you a lesson."

"Why, Elizabeth, that was wonderful!" Amy exclaimed.

"But I saw you in the garden," he said. "You were drinking champagne and Uncle Renzo was singing from *Aïda* and pushing you on the swing."

The sharp tone came back into Elizabeth's voice. "You're talking that nonsense again, I see. Well, Norman, there was some insanity on my mother's side."

"Aunt Elizabeth, I've never been to Italy in my life, but I was walking down the Old Appian Way with Larkey and when we returned she had to rush back into the house because you were all there and Monk was coming and she was late."

"Oh," chortled Amy, "I recall that night only too well. Remember, Elizabeth, when Monk made that terrible fuss?"

"Amy, you are not to encourage him in this lunacy."

"I'm not encouraging him in anything," Amy said. "I'm just thinking of that night when Monk got so angry he slapped Larkey's face."

Norman grabbed her arm. She screamed, "He's hurting me!"

"That is nothing compared to what I'm going to do to you if you continue along these lines," Elizabeth said.

Norman released Amy's arm. "O.K., Aunt Elizabeth," he said. "O.K., the whole thing was my imagination, and my mind is

83

playing tricks. Just tell me what happened to Larkey that night."

"How in God's name would I remember? It's over forty years ago."

"I remember everything," said Amy.

"I'll wager a thousand to one you don't." Elizabeth glared at her and Amy shook her head. "And then again, maybe I don't."

"Aunt Elizabeth, could you just answer one question?"

"Only if you stop talking this drivel."

"Why do you have to go into the back room to smoke marijuana? Can't you do it anywhere else in the apartment?"

"Foolish boy. What would happen if we were raided?"

"Who's going to raid you?"

She stared at him, shook her head back and forth and tsk-tsk-tsked. Before he could ask the question again, she said, "By the way, Norman, why did you come back?"

He was startled. "Oh, I realized I'd forgotten to ask you if you needed anything. The door was unlocked."

"Unlocked!" she shouted at Amy. "You left the door unlocked."

"Look," said Norman, "why don't I call you tomorrow and then you can let me know what you need?"

"Fabulous idea, darling," Elizabeth said. "Good night. Have a good rest. And we too shall go to sleep—perchance to dream—"

"Ay, there's the rub," Norman said, without even thinking.

"Amy," Elizabeth said, ignoring him, "Make sure the door is locked this time. And when you do, I have a quiz for you that you'll never guess in five hundred years—R.L."

As Norman walked out, he realized all four cats were once again sitting on the table and staring at him.

10

"Hello, stranger," Sharon greeted him the next day at work. "Why so gloomy?"

Norman handed her the note, which she read aloud:

> TO: NORMAN DICKENS
> FROM: ELLIOTT PERRY
> I want to see you in my office at 10
> A.M. sharp today.

She looked at him questioningly.

"It's because I was out all yesterday afternoon," he said.

"Where'd you go?"

"To my aunts' house. I had to be there while they had a phone installed."

"You mean they didn't have a telephone? They might as well be working here."

Norman laughed "Sharon, can we have lunch today?"

"I'd love it."

"Assuming Mr. Perry doesn't fire me at ten o'clock."

"He wouldn't dare. He can rant his heart out, but they'll never get another one like you for the kind of money they're paying. How many people understand five languages?"

"Four."

"Four people?"

"No, four languages."

"Well, I'm including English. That's a language, isn't it?"

"Barely." He smiled.

"Norman, there's a whole side to you I never imagined existed." She paused and smiled. "Your front and back aren't so bad either."

At one minute before ten Norman walked to Perry's office. Miss Prentiss looked up from her crossword puzzle long enough to sneer and wave him in. This morning, with her head encased in a black turban, she looked less like a dried apricot and more like a prune.

Perry was at his desk, turned completely around in his chair, his back to Norman, and talking on the telephone. He turned his head for a second, saw Norman, and wheeled around again. "What!" he exclaimed, then whispered something into the telephone and hung up. He turned to face Norman and put on his eyeglasses.

"Well, what do you have to say for yourself today, Norman?"

"I . . ."

"No, let me say it to save wear and tear on the nerves. I could easily recommend your dismissal for what you did yesterday. Mr. Donald and Mr. Worthman wouldn't give it a second thought."

"Mr. Perry . . ."

"Don't be rude. Let me finish. You took more than half a day off, for which you can be sure you'll be amply docked." He stared into Norman's eyes. "You don't look as though it concerns you too much. Does it, Norman?"

"Yes, Mr. Perry, it concerns me a great deal."

"Well, you don't look it, but then appearances are always deceiving with you, aren't they?" Norman didn't answer. "I said, 'Aren't they?' "

"If you say so, sir."

"Don't act bored with me. I can still throw you out."

Norman stood up. "Mr. Perry, if that's what you feel you want to do, then I'll pack my things."

"Well, well, look at the independence the young lad has suddenly developed."

Norman made for the door.

"Where are you going?"

"Is that all, sir?"

"No, that is not all, sir!" Perry mimicked. "Sit down. I don't give a flying saucer how sick your aunt is, or whoever you're supposed to be attending. I want a day's work around here from you. Do you understand?" He removed his glasses and polished them by licking on the lenses and then drying them with a bandanna kerchief from his breast pocket. "There will be no more excuses, Norman." He glanced pointedly at Norman's legs and Norman crossed them. Perry leaped up and started to scream, "I've never liked your goddamn superior attitude. One more infraction and you're through!" Norman stared at him. "That's all, Dickens. Now get out!"

Back at his desk, Norman was surprised that he wasn't upset. Was it because Perry was so ridiculous? Or because Larkey had put him into a new dimension and everything else mattered less?

At the elevator at noon Sharon told him, "We can take a little extra time for lunch today."

"Maybe you can, Sharon, but Mr. Perry made it very clear I have to go by the book from now on."

"Mr. Perry left ten minutes ago, and I heard from one of the girls who heard it from Miss Prentiss that he's gone for the weekend. Skiing, if you can believe it."

They went to Giambelli's and lunch was expensive, but then, Norman figured, life might turn out to be shorter than he'd originally planned.

Over the first glass of wine Sharon told him: She was twenty-three, had been a prelaw major at Radcliffe, was Manhattan-born from a family of well-to-do doctors, had been married at twenty-one to a young land developer, lived in Florida for the ten months of the marriage—until the developer landed another woman—divorced at twenty-two, that Norman was the only man she'd been to bed with besides her husband, Norman being by far the better of the two, that her hobbies were sculpting and betting on horses, and that she hadn't the faintest idea what she was doing at the Donworth Company—nor, for that matter, what *he* was doing there. He couldn't think of a sensible answer.

Over the second glass of wine he desultorily answered questions about himself, telling her little more than she already knew about him—that he spent the winter months watching football and movies on TV, the summer months playing baseball with a team of strangers in Central Park, and related to practically nobody.

Over the third glass of wine he began telling her about Amy and Elizabeth, frustrated that words could never capture the absurd contrast between the fabulous Gould sisters and the two women who lived in that stifling clutter downtown.

He ordered the entire meal in Italian.

"Well, you really put your languages to use," she said.

"Personally, I think it was a little pretentious of me."

"Where did you learn all those languages, Norman?"

"I studied French and Spanish in school, and my mother tutored me in German after school. And my father was originally from Italy. Both my parents spoke Italian around the house."

"Italian? You're the most Waspish—"

He smiled. "I'm more Italian than anything else. And speaking of Italy . . ." He told her about his experiences in the garden off Via Appia Antica, leaving out pertinent portions about Larkey.

"Norman, this is astonishing. If I didn't know you— I don't know you that well, but well enough to be sure you're not crazy. I never heard anything like it. Are you sure you weren't smoking along with your aunts?"

He smiled. "I smoked marijuana once in Vietnam and didn't like it and never tried it again. I'm the squarest person you'll ever meet, Sharon."

She took his hand. "If you're square, then the world is making a mistake being round."

The waiter put cannelloni in front of them, and for several minutes they ate silently.

"You know what, Norman? I have an uncle who's a psychiatrist. Dr. Frederic Morgan. Maybe you've heard of him. He's been quoted in all kinds of articles."

"I don't know that I need a psychiatrist yet."

"Oh, I'm not suggesting you go into analysis. I'd just like you to talk to him. He's doing a book about psychic phenomena and he'd love to hear your story, and maybe he could give you some advice. I'll make sure he doesn't charge you for the session. That'll be my Christmas present to you." She sounded like Norman now talking to Elizabeth and Amy. "I'll call him this afternoon. You know, Norman, you've talked more during this lunch than in the whole year we've known each other."

The sun outside warmed the freezing air. On the way back to the office she said, "How do you pronounce that dessert again?"

"Zabaglione. Rhymes with 'hobble Tony.' And you roll the 'l' a little." He felt giddy. Too much wine, he thought, putting his arm around Sharon's waist.

At the elevator she kissed him. "Thanks for the elegant lunch."

He looked at his watch. One thirty-five. "I hope you were right about Perry," he said.

On spotting him, Barbara said, "Norman, Miss Prentiss was mad as hell. She said Mr. Perry told her to keep tabs on you, and she wanted to know if I'd seen you. I said you were back at your desk at one, but then you got sick and went to the men's room. Was that O.K.?"

He put his arms around her and kissed her. She shook her head several times. "Norman, what's happened to you?"

He hung his coat up and walked over to Miss Prentiss' desk. "I hear you were looking for me, Miss Prentiss."

"Yes, I was," she said icily, and he was amazed at how close he came to smacking her across the mouth. "Mr. Perry told me to keep an eye on you."

"Well, Miss Prentiss, can you manage your crossword puzzle with just the other eye?"

"Why, how dare you? How dare you speak to me that way?"

"You'd be amazed at what I would dare," he said. "Does Mr. Perry know you spend most of your days doing puzzles?" He smiled and strolled away, not believing what he'd just said.

At four thirty Sharon rushed into his office excitedly. "Norman, Uncle Fred can see you tonight. Isn't that terrific? He says he's free from five fifteen to six, and he's dying to meet you."

"Sure, it isn't often a psychiatrist sees a bona-fide nut."

11

Dr. Fredric Morgan was in his late sixties, very dapper, tall, tweedy. He smoked a pipe, and Norman thought he was one of the few people he'd ever seen on whom a pipe looked authentic.

He smiled. "We're in luck. I think the moon must be full, but my next patient canceled too, so I can give you two sessions for the price of none."

Norman sat in an armchair facing Dr. Morgan in an identical chair.

"Well, Norman, Sharon says you have one hell of a story for me."

"Sir, do psychiatrists normally talk like this?"

"If psychiatrists knew how to do something normally they would have picked another profession," said Dr. Morgan. "And you don't have to call me sir. My name is Fred."

"Yes, Fred." And Norman, in a burst of nonstop talking, told Fred the story of his life, of Amy and Elizabeth, from his early memories to the present, leaving out only the details about Larkey.

Fred smiled. "Do you always talk this much?"

"It's possible I haven't talked this much in my whole life."

"I know. Sharon told me. Well, Norman, what do we do about you? First of all, it's a little early for me to tell whether you're experiencing any kind of psychic phenomenon. I'd have to hear about more episodes, assuming there are more. For the moment, we'll exclude the possibility and deal with the real world. Since I don't know your aunts, I can't judge whether they're senile. Certainly, they're living in some kind of fantasy world. Those voices you've heard outside the door which you think are from the past are most likely from the past. But it isn't you looking back. They are looking back and reliving a time when they were young and beautiful and happy. It's out of *their* fantasy, not yours. Relax on that point.

"You say the apartment was spacious and had dignity the last time you saw it eight years ago and you can't understand why they chopped it off that way and live in this unbelievable clutter. But, Norman, eight years ago was the day of your mother's funeral. Doesn't it occur to you that your mother's death was the perfect moment for the beginning of their incredible deterioration? It was like part of them dying, probably much worse than the loss of their house or money.

"Now, more evidence of their infantile behavior are their grocery orders—the items naughty children would order from a store if their parents were not around to see that they ate something more nourishing. Apply the same principle to all their little word games, the laughter that stops abruptly, the secrets, the double meanings. Little children, with a house full of cats and crackerjacks. They're doing everything a parent would not approve of."

"O.K., Doctor, but now explain my trips into the garden in Italy."

"I'll try. Who knows what may turn up in the future, but for the moment, this is what I think: You say you're extremely sensitive to any kind of drugs or pills. Well, let's assume these aunts of yours are smoking marijuana in that back room. Because of your sensitivity you may be affected by the fumes. Also, you may be in a state of suspended emotion. What I mean is, a state of shock. I know if I ever walked into an apartment like that I might have a heart attack. Now, this suspended emotion, combined with the fumes, could send you into a dreamlike state. In the first case you said you fainted. The second time you were knocked on the head by a candlestick. The third time you were not knocked out, but you knocked yourself out, in effect. You were fascinated by that magic place. You wanted to go back. I don't blame you. It sounds great."

"Doctor—excuse me—Fred. I'll accept all that. But how do you account for my seeing people I've never met, walking down a road I've never seen, visiting a tomb?"

"Easily. Your parents could have told you things you've forgotten in your conscious mind and they've suddenly come back to you. You've also probably seen pictures."

"Well, I was looking at our old photo album the other day and I saw my aunts and my uncle, but can I tell you something in confidence?"

Fred laughed. "You're not on the Mike Douglas show. If you can't tell a psychiatrist something in confidence, who can you tell?"

Norman sat thoughtfully for a few minutes. Then he told Fred about Larkey.

"Fred, I never saw a picture of her anywhere."

"It's very likely, Norman, that if Larkey left such an impression on your aunts she also left an impression on your mother—or father—and they could have told you about her when you were a child. You could easily have heard about her black hair and blue eyes. It's a combination people always talk about. The first thing Sharon told me about you was that you have black hair and blue eyes."

"But why would I fall in love with Larkey?"

"Norman, from what you've said about your relationships with women since your disappearing fiancée, I'd say you're scared to death to commit yourself again. With Larkey there's no need to be scared. You're ripe for fantasies about women and love."

Norman blushed, then smiled. He wondered whether Sharon had told Fred anything about Wednesday night. "Fred, I'll go along with everything, but I'm still not sure what to do."

Fred shook his head. "Norman, I'm going to indulge myself in a luxury psychiatrists can't afford and give you some advice. As attractive as that garden is, as beautiful as Larkey is, they're not real. Find your garden and your Larkey in this world. Easy, right?" He laughed again. "But more important, if you value your well-being, you'll cut out your visits to that insane asylum. Those ladies and their cats and furniture and infantile games will destroy you."

"But I can't just let them die."

"No, you can't. But you're also not your brother's keeper, nor your aunts'. Point out to them that they should be in what we euphemistically call a senior citizens' home. They are obviously incapable of taking care of themselves. If you need help in that area, I can make some suggestions. It needn't be a financial burden on you. With Medicare and Social Security, it probably wouldn't cost them a thing."

"Do you think they would ever move out of that place?"

"It's their business, not yours, Norman. If they want to help themselves and move, then you help them. If they don't, then why should you kill yourself? That's what you'll be doing, you know. And on that happy note I am sorry to tell you your time is up or my next patient will fire me. I'd like to talk to you again sometime, Norman. Soon. Call me. If you persist in this madness, at the very least I'd like to hear what's happening." He smiled and stood up. "You know something? I can't remember when I've spent a busier hour and a half." He shook Norman's hand.

"Fred," Norman asked, "do you think I'm— Do you think I—"

"Do I think you're crazy or need therapy? You might be a good candidate sometime, but I don't think you think you're ready for it. You know, for somebody who's never had one session, you're amazingly candid."

"Isn't that how you're supposed to be?"

"Of course, but are people ever how they're supposed to be? It's taken some of my patients years to get to the stage you're at." He put his hand on Norman's shoulder. "Dump those aunts. Gently, of course. In the area of communication you seem to be doing fine. But if everything gets too much for you and you're in the market to spend fifty bucks a shot three times a week for five years, I'm your man. Meantime, get a little rest and sunshine and see some 1973 girls. You know, you could do worse than my niece." He winked. "I give relatives a discount, by the way, even those by marriage."

Norman smiled. "You're a nice man, Fred."

"Get out of here. You're beginning to sound like my patients."

Norman had to tell him. "Fred, I wish you'd been my father."

Fred stared at him, then laughed. "If I'd been your father, Norman, today you'd be an astigmatic, semibald orthodontist with watery brown eyes. Now get the hell out."

12

Norman entered his building just as Mrs. Shomer and her companion, Ellen, were coming in.

"Norman, where have you been keeping yourself?"

"What?" Norman was stunned. What was wrong with the way she was speaking? It had sounded like "Normarrn, wherre harve yor beern keerpirng yourrselrf?"

"Mrs. Shomer, are you chewing something?"

"Chewing? No, why do you ask?"

Another revelation, he thought. Mrs. Shomer, whom he'd

known for three years, whom he'd spoken to on a hundred occasions, and he'd just noticed how funny she talked. Every word had r's in it.

"Well, honey, where have you been hiding this week?"

"Oh, Mrs. Shomer, I have a sick aunt downtown and I've been going there every day to help her out."

"You're a fine boy, Norman. Always helping people. Listen, I have a dripping in my sink in the kitchen. Do you think you'll have a little time to come in and fix it?"

He bit his lip. There must have been three hundred r's in that last sentence. Norman, he thought, where has your head been? Maybe I've been living in a fantasy world all my life until now. "Mrs. Shomer, if I have some free time this weekend, I'll knock on your door. It depends on how my aunt is feeling."

He was trying so hard to force down the exploding laughter in his head that it took several attempts to get the key into the lock. By this time Fulcho was screaming his lungs out just inside the door, and when Norman got it open he leaped up onto his arm and hung there.

"Whyr, herlo, Furlchor, dird your harve a nirce dayr?"

The cat dropped off his arm and stared at him incredulously. Norman laughed, scooped the cat up and rubbed noses with him. He was purring madly.

"O.K., baby, kidneys coming up, but first I have to make a call."

He dialed, heard the telephone picked up on the other end, then Amy's voice faintly from a distance, as if through a tunnel.

"Hello, Aunt Amy?"

"Hello?" came the distant voice. "Hello?"

"Aunt Amy, is something wrong with the telephone?"
Nothing.

Norman muttered to himself, "Damn telephone company. It took eight years—eight years—to get a phone back into that house and on the second day it's out of order. He dialed again and once more the telephone was picked up and again he heard Aunt Amy's far-off voice.

"Aunt Amy!" he shouted, so loud that Fulcho leaped off the table and raced away into the bathroom.

Now her voice came through clearly. "Hello?"

"Aunt Amy, it's Norman. Was something wrong with your phone?"

"No, Norman, I was holding the receiver the wrong way. I was speaking into the hearing part." She giggled. "Isn't that funny?"

"Hilarious. Look, I just got home, but I'll be down there soon. There's a supermarket open late around here. Is there anything you need?"

"Elizabeth, do you need anything?" she called.

He heard Aunt Elizabeth's commanding voice in the background. "A can of Ovaltine and four egg rolls. And tell him to get something for himself and I'll pay for it."

Fred was certainly right about their eating habits. He looked around for Fulcho.

"O.K., Aunt Amy, I'll see you soon."

"Fulcho! Come out of the bathroom. Please. Kidneys!"

The cat crept cautiously toward the kitchen and stopped a few feet away from Norman with one paw upraised.

"Come on, Fulch, I wasn't yelling at *you*." He picked him up and put him onto the counter. Fulcho sniffed Norman's nose, then relaxed and began to groom himself as his master cut his kidneys.

Norman showered, then put on his best suit and aftershave. Inspecting himself in the mirror, he thought, As though it matters. If I see Larkey I'll be in different clothes, anyway.

They were seated at the table when he walked in, Elizabeth in a red lace robe, its hood over her head, Amy in a faded pink ruffled nightgown.

"Do you like the way we look, darling?" Amy asked. "We dressed up for you, you know."

"Oh . . . uh . . . very nice, very nice."

Elizabeth laughed. "Oh, yes, I can certainly tell from your

expression that you think we look nice—about as nice as an earthquake!"

Norman blushed.

"Elizabeth," said Amy, "you're always minimizing us these days. Norman, speaking of nice, you smell so lovely. Are you wearing cologne?"

"Did you find Signe?" he asked.

She blinked and stared at him.

Elizabeth answered. "No. She must have got out of the house and run away. If she were here, she'd have come out for food by now." She looked up toward the ceiling. "She's gone. Good riddance. Now let's eat. I'm famished."

The two old women munched their egg rolls wordlessly and Norman leaned against the Austrian stove and studied them.

After they were finished he helped Elizabeth to her bed. Then he walked into the kitchen wondering how he was going to get into that back room.

"Aunt Amy, you look very tired. Why don't you and Aunt Elizabeth take a nap and I'll let myself out."

"Bless you," Elizabeth said. "The nights get kind of long around here, you know, not that I'm complaining!"

"I tell you what, Aunt Elizabeth," he said, looking at the broken TV set. "Why don't I get you and Amy a new TV set— in color? There's so much you could see—"

"We don't need it. We don't need to spend that kind of money."

"It wouldn't cost you anything," he said. "It would be my present to you. *That's* going to be my Christmas present."

"Oh, you foolish boy," Elizabeth called. "Don't waste your money. Our needs are so simple, so astonishingly simple. You're such a good boy, Norman."

Wait till I spring that senior citizens' home on you, he thought.

He helped Amy into bed and covered her with some of the old fur coats. For about half an hour he drifted aimlessly around downtown, then he went back to the apartment and entered silently. Albert, perched on the shelf above the sink, spotted him and meowed softly. Instantly, all four cats surrounded him, staring. He put his finger to his lips, then tiptoed to the dining room. The loud snoring reassured him and he very quietly pushed open the door to the back room and walked in. Tonight he smelled basil.

A full moon shone on the garden, causing the pond to sparkle with an other-world light and the swans to glow as though they were made of spun glass. One black one sailed silently toward Norman, then let out a call that reminded him of Elizabeth and Amy's cats. He walked up to the edge of the pond and looked at the swan. It had tiny white furrows on its brow and an intelligent expression. Its beady eyes stared at him. Norman felt paralyzed at the side of the pond until the swan opened its beak, gave a soft coo at him and sailed majestically away.

He shivered. No, he thought, my imagination is running amok. Then he began to laugh. *If I can land in another world, why can't anything else be possible?* Signe had never been found. Signe . . . Cigno . . . Cigno was Italian for swan. Cygne was French for swan. Well, so what? But he couldn't stop trembling.

There wasn't another sound in the garden as he padded the long distance to the house through grass that was so thick that it was difficult to walk. Conflicting sweet smells assailed him. Finally he reached the house and walked up the flight of white marble steps.

How do I get to Larkey without Elizabeth and Amy seeing me? Well, maybe they won't be here. They're sleeping.

He knocked on the door, noting in the light reflecting from the cut crystal panels on either side that he was wearing an outfit of maroon chamois, trimmed with jewels. I must compliment my tailor, if I ever meet him, he thought.

The heavy carved door was opened by the manservant who had served the champagne on the previous day.

"Signor?"

"Please tell Signorina Barberini that Mr. Dickens has come to call on her."

The servant admitted Norman into the immense entrance hall

and disappeared. The floor on which Norman stood was a design of squares, octagons and hearts within ever-widening circles, all in different shades of marble—maroon and pink and white and purple. Ahead of him was the kind of double winding staircase he had seen in his grandfather's Fifth Avenue house. The walls were covered with murals, with panels of geometric decorations above them, and then he looked at the ceiling and gasped. Dozens of panels, each with a hand-painted classical scene, filled the area. Norman wondered whether this would one day be a museum. Maybe, he thought, it is *now* in 1973. Ornate furniture lined the hallway and the air smelled of peonies.

A burst of noise from the left preceded the appearance of Larkey, running toward him, followed by Elizabeth, Amy and Maria, each of them wearing a tiny button with a hand-painted flower, obviously gifts from Larkey. Larkey was flushed, and as she got closer the smell of peonies became stronger. The three other girls were chattering in Italian, but he wasn't listening.

Larkey came right up to him. "Norman," she whispered, "you must not stay. There has been a change of plan."

"Why, hello again, Signor Dickens," Elizabeth said. "What a pleasant surprise." Now she switched to English. "I hope you came to see *all* of us."

"I don't really think he did," said Maria in German. "Not from the way he's staring at Larkey." She smiled. Hello, Mother, Norman said in his head.

"This is surely not the night for anybody to be staring at Larkey," said Amy, looking back toward the doorway through which they had come.

As if on signal, a tall man strode through and came toward them. In his early thirties, Norman guessed, handsome in a suave kind of way, with very black hair, a mustache, a hooked Roman nose and dark hostile eyes staring at him.

"Well, is somebody going to introduce me to this stranger?" he said testily to the girls.

"Oh, of course, Monk," said Elizabeth. "This is our new friend, Signor Norman Dickens."

"Whose new friend?" asked Monk Abruzzi.

"Why, our new friend. He is a friend to all of us," said Amy.

"Perhaps one of you more than the others?" He glared at Larkey, who lowered her eyes, and Norman looked away from Abruzzi and stifled a gasp. On the bosom of Larkey's dress was the diamond stickpin Aunt Elizabeth had given him the other night, its prismatic lights burning into him.

"Signor," Abruzzi said to him, "do you find something interesting on the dress of my *fidanzata?*"

"Yes," Norman said. "That is a very handsome jewel." Larkey blushed.

"She certainly is. Now, will you ladies please excuse us? I would like to have a word with Signor— I'm afraid I've forgotten your name."

"Dickens. Norman Dickens."

"I have read all the works of your illustrious namesake," said Abruzzi as he took Norman's arm and led him to the room from which he'd come.

Through carved gold doors Norman entered a drawing room whose elegance shamed that of the entrance hall. The floor was shades of green marble and blue alabaster, with rugs from the Orient, tables and chairs from the Renaissance, a piano that looked as though it had been sculpted. The walls were panels of religious murals separated by green velvet, and the ceiling was a larger version of the gold doors. From the ceiling hung a treasure of crystal and gold, lighting the room.

"Won't you have a seat, Signor Dickens," said Abruzzi, smiling. Norman knew he was supposed to accept this as cordiality, but the smile barely concealed the man's hostility. He sat on a dark blue velvet couch. In front of him was a long table duplicating, in a hundred colors of marble, the center of the Sistine Chapel ceiling.

"Can we offer you some wine, Signor?"

"Yes, please," said Norman, wondering when the girls were going to come in. Abruzzi pushed a button under the table and a butler entered from one of the panels in the wall carrying a tray which contained a bottle of red wine and two glasses.

Abruzzi waved him away and poured a bit into Norman's glass, then stared at him. "Signor, is it not the custom of foreigners to taste first?"

Norman sipped, nodded and Abruzzi filled both glasses, then took a large gulp, followed by a gasping noise of satisfaction. "The Ferromonte vineyards are the best in Italy," he said. "For years I have tried to buy them, but they refuse to sell. I think they think me crass." He laughed. It was an ugly laugh.

"Now, Signor Dickens, tell me about yourself."

What is this? Norman thought. Stiffly, he said, "What would you like to know, Signor Abruzzi?"

Abruzzi glinted evilly. "Call me Monk."

"Thank you, Monk," Norman articulated through gritted teeth.

Monk caught the meaning and smiled. "Very well, Norman, I shall merely ask you questions. Where are you from?"

"The United States."

"And what brings you here?"

The fantasies of my crazy aunts, who aren't my aunts yet. The escape from my own dismal life. The fumes of marijuana. What would you say, Monk, if I told you the stickpin on your beloved's chest is in a cigarette box on a table four thousand miles and forty-five years from here?

"Signor, you seem to be drifting."

"I am sorry. I am here on holiday. I was born in New York City. I am twenty-six years of age." He could barely control his anger. "What more would you like to know?"

"You have not told me what you are doing here."

"I am here on the invitation of the young ladies inside."

"And where did you meet those young ladies?"

"I came upon the garden by accident."

Monk burst into loud, sarcastic laughter, then cut it off abruptly. "And you seriously expect me to believe that one can just chance onto the estate of the Ferromonte family—one of the most famous in all of Italy?"

Norman stood up and upset his wine glass. "Signor, I don't

seriously expect you to believe anything, nor do I really give a damn. I am not here to visit with you nor to make your acquaintance, and as far as I'm concerned this interview is over."

"Sit down," commanded Monk.

Norman glared at him.

"Sit down," Monk said more gently. "I have, perhaps, been rude. Now I wish to speak with you seriously."

"Had you been joking till now?"

Monk smiled and stroked his mustache. "Please sit. Good. Now, let me tell you something about myself. I was born in Urbino thirty-four years ago in such poverty as you in the United States cannot even imagine. At the age of seven I was picking grapes in rich men's arbors to help my father and mother earn enough to keep us alive. Two of my brothers and one of my sisters died of starvation. Does this shock you in your lavish bejeweled costume of animal skin? I slaved and I stole, but mostly I learned. I learned that it is not necessary for a person to starve, that so long as one man was rich another man could become rich. I became acquainted with powerful men who rule most of the world from that much maligned island which rests quietly under the toes of this country. I did necessary services for them until I earned my way up. I am now, and I say this with no arrogance, one of the four or five most powerful men in this country." His eyes glowed with satisfaction and he smiled broadly. "Have you heard anybody speak of me before?"

"No."

"My power and influence are conceded by one and all. But very few know how far it actually extends. Would it surprise you to hear that I could have you killed inside one hour without a trace, with no possible connection to me?"

We think he's working for the Mafia. Amy's ridiculous words to Pearlie leaped up at Norman now and he smiled.

"You smile. I am glad to see you understand me. Now we come to the present. I have arranged to marry Larkey. In fact, our wedding is only three days from now."

Norman wiped his hands along his thighs to keep calm.

Monk stood up, walked over to a sideboard and removed a wine glass into which he poured more wine for Norman, who drank it down.

"Nothing will stop this marriage between Larkey and myself," he continued. "Nothing and no one. You see, Norman, I am not only powerful, I am also not stupid. When the servant announced you before, he said a gentleman had come to call on Signorina Barberini. Not on all the girls—on Larkey. I observed the way Larkey looked at you and the animal way in which you looked at her. Do you think you convinced me you were staring at a jewel on her breast? You would like to touch that breast, wouldn't you?" He slammed his hand on the table. "Wouldn't you?"

"The thought hadn't entered my mind," said Norman very quietly.

Monk smiled. "American humor, eh? Well, make sure the thought doesn't enter your mind in the future. Let me continue. Last night Larkey was very late coming in for dinner. She said she had been out walking with a friend and had forgotten the time. But, you see, I already had a report about the 'friend' she'd been with at the tomb of Cecelia Metella, a very accurate description of you. You are an easy person to describe, Norman. My influence, you may note, covers many areas and very little of what interests me ever escapes me. If I cared—and I don't really —within one hour I could find out every detail about your life, your arrival in Italy, and your purpose, without your telling me a word."

Just try that one, Monk, Norman thought. Will your spies come up with a beaut.

"So, Norman, to conclude: I have nothing against you personally. Yes, as a matter of fact, I do. Why lie? But I am feeling magnanimous because my wedding is only three days off. Therefore, when you leave this house tonight—and I will give you ample time to leave gracefully—I expect you will never appear here again."

"This isn't your house. It belongs to the Ferromonte—"

"Every house in Italy is my house, Norman. Yes, you may return here. Any time after the wedding . . . and any time I am not here with Signora Abruzzi, whom I shall possess within seventy-two hours. Does that bother you, Norman?"

Norman never got the chance to answer. The door opened and Lorenzo Ferromonte came in.

"Oh, there you are, Monk, and Norman Dickens, is it? How nice to see you again. Monk, I did not know you and Norman were acquainted."

"We are better acquainted than you would imagine, Renzo."

Renzo raised an eyebrow, stared at Norman, then at Monk. "Well, If I am interrupting something, I don't care. It is time for dancing, and the ladies are impatient. Shall we adjourn to the ballroom?"

Monk stood up. "Certainly. Norman, would you care to join us before you rush off to the city?"

"It will be a pleasure," said Norman flatly, and Renzo stared at him again.

"You know something," said Renzo to Monk, "Norman and Larkey both have blue eyes and black hair. They could be related."

"I have no doubt," said Monk dryly, then walked out to the entrance hall.

Renzo took Norman's elbow and led him out. "I hope you don't mind that I call you Norman," he said. He realized that Renzo was taller and blonder and much younger than he'd seemed in the old wedding pictures. He found too that he could no longer picture this person as the villain who had broken Elizabeth's heart. And he wondered what Renzo would be like in 1973, had he and Aunt Elizabeth stayed married.

The ballroom was directly across the hall from the drawing room and about four times its size, with a magnificent stained-glass ceiling. One entire long wall was also stained glass, containing portraits of the Ferromonte ancestors, with names and birth dates.

Belying all this Old World elegance was the music—the

Charleston—wildly played and wildly danced by more than two dozen people. Center of attention was Elizabeth, who managed to dance with every man in the room. This having been accomplished, she retired to a round of applause, relinquishing the floor to a tiny little beauty in a fluffy white gown who did the Black Bottom with the young man Norman had seen with Renzo and the girls on his first trip into the garden. Soon the other dancers gathered around and watched. Then Renzo switched with the little beauty's partner and so in turn did all the other men in the room, with the exception of Monk Abruzzi. Norman saw him leaning against a Donatello statue of a young man and holding Larkey's hand. The deep red of her dress accentuated the absence of color in her face as she talked earnestly and rapidly to Monk, who simply nodded. For a second, Norman's eyes locked with Larkey's, then she quickly turned away. Monk looked over at Norman and beckoned him to join them. Norman ignored him and took a glass of champagne from a passing butler.

Renzo approached him. "Do you dance, Norman?"

"Not this dance."

"I am surprised. This is an American dance. I thought all Americans have rhythm."

You heard wrong, Renzo, Norman thought. All *black* Americans have rhythm.

"There have to be exceptions to prove the rule, Renzo. You dance better than any American I've ever known."

"Thank you. Perhaps you would like to meet some of the other girls here? How about the one in white?"

"Oh, no, thanks. I'll just stand and watch. I'm supposed to leave soon."

"Oh, I hope you have not been too intimidated by our local gangster."

"He seems to think I'm trying to take Larkey away from him."

"Well, is that not the truth?"

"I don't know what's the truth. But I guess, for all concerned, it's best if I leave."

"Don't leave, Norman. The Gould girls are taken with you and I would very much like to have you as our guest. Monk may be very powerful politically, but he still cannot tell me who comes and goes in my house."

"But he can make Larkey suffer, can't he?"

"I'm sure Monk is capable of making anybody suffer. I tell you what, why not pretend to leave? Go out by the front door, then turn left and go to the rear of the house, where you will see a grove of cypress trees. Follow the sounds of water and you will come to a fountain. Wait there.

"Monk is not going to stay long and he leaves Rome tomorrow. He expects to transact business"—Renzo raised his eyes skyward—"in Palermo over the weekend. There is nothing like a few killings to whet a bridegroom's appetite just before his nuptials, I hear." He smiled wryly. "After he leaves, I will come to get you. By that time a room will have been prepared for you, and I would consider it an insult if you did not stay as our guest for the weekend."

"Who is your guest for the weekend?" asked Monk, stopping directly in front of them with his arm around Larkey, whose lips were trembling.

"I was just telling Norman it is a shame he must leave tonight and that I would deem it an honor if he were to be our guest for some future weekend."

Monk smiled. "Yes, what a sensible idea. We have come over so Larkey can say goodbye to Norman. We certainly wouldn't want him detained any longer than necessary."

Norman stared into Larkey's eyes and wondered how he could tell her. She blinked away tears, then extended an icy hand. "It has been a pleasure meeting you, Norman," she said stiffly, "and I sincerely hope that on your next visit to Italy we may have the privilege again."

Norman nodded and then kissed her hand.

"How quaint you Americans are," Monk said sarcastically, and Norman was about to reply in kind when he was distracted by the wild dancing of a couple just behind them.

The tiny little beauty in the fluffy white gown caught Norman's eye and winked at him, then danced away.

Norman shook Renzo's hand, thanked him for his hospitality and turned around and left the house. He was trembling almost too much to walk. The tiny winking beauty in the ballroom had been Pearlie Gish.

He didn't know how long he stood there on the front steps, but he was finally able to move. On the way to the fountain he passed the stained-glass wall of the ballroom and saw the wild movements within, but he couldn't make out any of the people. If only he could get one more look. No, he didn't really want to be sure. The ceiling of the ballroom, he realized, was also the roof and he wondered how long that ceiling would last in New York City in 1973. And, ironically, how much longer Norman Dickens was going to last in 1973—or 1928.

The fountain contained three marble figures restraining some kind of monster, from whose mouth sprang a jet of water accompanied by vertical spouts all around. Norman sat on a filigree metal bench and stared at the splashing water, which, no matter what the rhythm, seemed to keep time to the music he heard from the house. Off in the distance the could just see the vague outlines of the olive groves set against lush hills.

The stars here seemed more crowded together than at home. I'm spending the weekend in Rome, he thought. Could be worse. Maybe Monk will die in a plane crash. Do many people fly in 1928? Maybe one of his enemies in Palermo will kill him. Maybe I will kill him.

He wasn't sure how much time had elapsed, or whether he'd dozed, but he was stunned to see Renzo standing in front of him.

"The villain of our piece has gone," said Renzo, sitting down next to him. "It is amazing, isn't it," he said, "how one man's problems can be another man's salvation."

Norman smiled. What was Renzo talking about?

"In case you think I've gone mad . . . you would give anything in the world to have Larkey, and I would give anything in the world not to have any woman. But it appears I am to have one. I have a problem. I do not see any sense in boring you with it. But I must marry. There has been too much gossip. My parents have given me the final ultimatum. This evening they telephoned from Milano and told me I must marry or be banished without a lira. I notice you do not inquire why."

Norman tried to keep his eyes noncommittal.

"Perhaps there is more awareness in you Americans than we have been led to believe." Especially, thought Norman, when I know how this race is going to finish. "Anyway, Norman, though we have barely talked, I consider you a friend. I do not invite everybody to spend the weekend at my home. And because of this, and because I do not really trust too many people, I wanted you to be first to know that I am about to propose marriage to Signorina Elizabeth Gould." He looked at Norman expectantly.

Norman smiled.

"You think this is a wise choice?" Renzo asked.

Now's your chance, Norman. One word from you and he could marry Maria and become your father.

"Yes," said Norman. "Any of the Gould sisters would be a wise choice."

"But Elizabeth seems the liveliest, the most sophisticated, the one most likely to understand." He paused and stared off at the fountain, then Norman noticed tears on his face. "It is very difficult for somebody like me, Norman. It is a difficulty you will never know, thank heaven. Come, let us go to the house."

I'm sorry you're not still my uncle, Norman thought. I'm sorry I never had a decent man related to me.

"Where did you meet the Gould sisters, Renzo?"

"They came to Rome on holiday a month ago. I was sitting on the Via Veneto one night as they pranced by, laughing, of course. It was actually Elizabeth who introduced herself—scandalous even in *your* country, I have heard. 'Signor,' she said, 'you are alone and we are three unescorted ladies, as you can see. Would you like to join our party and make us look respectable?' Her Italian was impeccable and I'd never heard any woman talk like this before. I was so impressed that I immediately got up and left with them, leaving a note behind for . . . the friend who was going to meet me there.

"They were so taken with me and I with them that I invited them to house-guest. They cabled their parents, who granted permission. Their father is rather distinguished, you know. I had feared he would say no. You may never have heard of Simon Gould in the United States, but he is one of London's most important entrepreneurs. He deals in metals and gems, and no lady of society anywhere in Europe would think of wearing a fur that did not come from the Gould company."

"Oh, a storekeeper," Norman said, smiling.

Renzo laughed out loud. "More than that. He has turned storekeeping into an industry, an art. He is a man who gives generously to the arts as well, and I believe you have people like him in your country. He is one of the few, as you say, storekeepers in history who is consulted regularly by leaders of several governments."

"Have you met the other Gould children?" Norman asked, aware too late of his slip.

"You know there are other Gould children?"

"Oh, no I just assumed the family was larger than the three sisters."

"Yes, there are several others. I am sure I will meet them at our wedding, assuming Elizabeth will have me."

As they passed the stained-glass wall Norman realized the dance was still going on. "Renzo, it might not be right for me to go in there."

"I told you, Monk is halfway to Rome by now."

"But what about his associates? Do you know that Monk has spies who report to him on Larkey's activities?"

"No, I did not know that, but I suppose it does not surprise me. I feel great sympathy for Larkey. It is ironic, but do you know she met Monk through the Gould family?"

"What?" Norman blinked.

"Simon Gould was in Rome three months ago on a business trip. He was lunching with Larkey and her parents—poor relations of one of his London executives—when his path crossed that of Monk. Monk, you see, is associated with quite a number of respectable people in Rome, some of whom do business with Simon Gould. Well, on their arrival in Rome last month the Gould sisters looked up Larkey and her family at their father's behest. And Larkey was added to the guest list of the Ferromonte household. Monk, of course, was delighted to add some respectable tone to his life. You see how paths cross and recross? I shouldn't be surprised—" He grabbed Norman's arm. "Norman, stay. Stay the summer with us. Maybe you too will marry one of the Gould sisters and we shall be brothers-in-law. Maria is the prettiest. She is only sixteen—"

Mr. and Mrs. Oedipus Dickens, Norman thought.

"I can't Renzo. I would very much like to stay, but I know I won't be here too long." *How do I know that?*

They were about to enter the house when Norman remembered something. "Renzo, inside, there's a tiny little girl in a white dress. Who is she?"

Renzo laughed. "Nobody knows. She just appeared and has everybody guessing. But she is such a pretty little thing. Like Cinderella at the ball."

They entered the house and Renzo signaled to a butler standing near the staircase. "Antonio, this is Mr. Dickens. Please escort him to his room." To Norman: "The dance will be ending soon. When all the guests have gone I will call you down and it will be just us, the Gould girls and Larkey—and we know none of *us* is a spy for Signor Abruzzi." He laughed and walked toward the ballroom.

The staircase was lined with marble statues, and at the top of the stairs was an enormous painting that resembled the work of Leonardo da Vinci. Well, thought Norman, maybe it's the real thing.

The room into which the butler showed him was, like all the others, marble floored. The enormous carved gold bed was set on a platform. The ceiling, like that in the entrance hall, was filled with painted murals in its panels. The bathroom was brown marble, with a sunken tub and gold fixtures. He walked to the double glass doors, opened them and stepped out onto a balcony, from which he could see the swans. The black one was calling out its soft mew as his eyes went beyond Signe and stared at the cluster of bushes that tied him to 1973.

He sat on the bed and noticed that on a low table next to him was a bottle of champagne chilling in a bucket. It was 1924 champagne, he saw, and wondered whether it was a good year.

He lay on the bed and studied the painted panels on the ceiling.

He was being shaken.

"Norman," said Renzo softly.

"I'm sorry. I guess I dozed."

"If you prefer to retire, I shall—"

"Is everybody gone?"

"Yes."

"Give me a few minutes and I'll join you downstairs. Where?"

"What?" asked Renzo.

"Where will you be downstairs? This is a very big house."

Renzo laughed. "Norman, you look as though you are used to big houses. We will be in the drawing room."

Norman raced into the bathroom and splashed water onto his face, then combed his hair with the carved ivory comb on the dressing table, stared at himself in the mirror for a long time and went downstairs.

He opened the door to the drawing room, and all four girls spotted him at the same time.

Larkey looked as though she was going to cry. She rushed over and took his hands.

"So *this* is the surprise," said Elizabeth. "What a wonderful one!"

"I'll bet it's a better surprise for *one* of us than for the rest," said Maria in French.

"Do you consider that humorous?" asked Amy.

"Oh, Lord," said Elizabeth. "Fill the brat with champagne and there's no shutting her up."

But Norman wasn't looking at them. He saw himself reflected in Larkey's eyes, and now she couldn't stop her tears.

"I thought I would never see you again," she whispered.

"So did I," he said.

She wiped her eyes and turned to the group. "I hope you will all excuse Norman and myself. Since we are never to see each other beyond this weekend, we have much to say."

Larkey led him up the stairs and into a room several doors down from his. The entire room was done in white. White marble floor, silk walls, white furniture, ermine on the bed and a cut-crystal and ivory chandelier. She led him to the balcony and they stood together, not speaking, for several minutes.

"There is where I first met you," said Norman, pointing at the garden.

"I have seen you always, Norman," she said and began to cry. He took her into his arms and she cried for a long time.

"Larkey, we can't just let this happen to us."

"There is nothing that can be done, my darling Norman. In three days I shall be Signora Abruzzi and shall never lay eyes on you again." She led him back into the room and waved her arm. "Virginal white, for the bride!" She laughed bitterly, then threw herself into his arms. "But not for him," she whispered.

They glided slowly to the bed. Larkey undid the top of her dress. "This you may have, my darling." Norman stared in disbelief. She removed the dress. "And this, and everything that is Larkey shall be yours, Norman." She kissed him again.

"I love you, Larkey, I'll always love you," he said as their bodies touched and ignited something in Norman that he'd never known was there.

They called each other's names over and over and then clung together silently, drowning in love they'd had no time to express.

"This must be what it's like to be born," he said.

"Norman," she whispered. "Norman, I am so filled with joy it would not matter if I died now. I shall love you forever."

They fell asleep together and when they woke made love again until they could see the pale light of morning trickling through the windows.

"Wouldn't it be beautiful if we'd conceived a child, Norman?" He kissed her. "He would never know until his deathbed, and then I would tell him."

He rubbed his nose against hers.

"Why do you do that? Is it an American custom?"

"You remind me of Fulcho," he said before he could catch himself.

"*Fuoco?* Fire?"

"No, no, not fire, Fulcho." Why had it never occurred to him, the language genius, how close to the Italian word for "fire" was his cat's name? Because until Larkey, lots of things had never occurred to him. "It's really very foolish," he said.

"Tell me, please."

"Fulcho is the name of my cat. I have a cat at home in New York. Have you Siamese cats in Italy?"

"Yes."

"Whenever he sees me he begins to purr and I rub noses with him," Norman said, smiling.

"Where did you get the name Fulcho? Does it mean something in English?"

"It doesn't mean anything," he said. "It just seemed right at the time."

"At the time? I do not understand."

"I bought him as a gift for somebody, and the first name that came into my head was Fulcho. It just seemed right at the time. And it seems right at this time to tell you I love you." How easily that comes out now, he thought.

"If he was a gift for somebody, why do you have him?"

"It's a long and boring story and I won't waste your time by telling it."

"Oh, Norman," she said, "I shall never be unhappy for as long as I am with you, for the little time we have left. You must leave soon."

"But Renzo has asked me to stay for the weekend. Monk will be away."

"Monk has changed his plans," she said. "He is coming here this morning for a visit before he leaves for Palermo. I am sure it is less to see me than to make sure you are not here. You must not be in this house."

"I could stay in my room."

"No, you must not even take a chance on being seen by the servants. Please, dearest, leave me and return later in the day. His airplane leaves at one o'clock in the afternoon."

"But Renzo will ask for me."

"I shall explain to Renzo, *everything*, if necessary. I can trust him." She began to tremble. "You must go, now!"

He dressed quickly in the dark, and as he was putting on his shoes his hand touched her dress on the floor and felt the stickpin. He switched on a small lamp at the side of the bed.

"Oh, my God! Norman." She covered her mouth and then pointed down. The ermine spread was stained with blood. "This I have given you," she said. "I do not know how I will explain it to my host." She laughed. "Oh, Norman, I am so happy I don't care."

He ran his hand over the glowing jewel on her dress.

"Larkey, where did you get this pin?"

"It belonged to my father, the prince. It was the only gift he ever gave my mother. She has given it to me to pass on to Signor Simon Gould as a gift for having introduced the family to Monk." She shook her head sadly. "People are to be given presents for that splendid introduction. Hm! Monday evening, before I leave this house to go to my new home, I shall give it to Elizabeth to present to her father. I would rather give it to you."

"You must keep your promise," he said, kissing her.

"*Arrivaderla*, Norman," she said.

It wasn't quite light as Norman padded across the lawn, tears running down his face. He touched them. Norman Dickens, he thought, who hasn't cried since he was a baby. As he reached the pond he heard the soft calling of the black swan and he stopped. She sailed over to him.

"Hello, Signe," he said.

The swan put its head against Norman's chest and rested its beak under his arm. Norman patted it on the head and tickled its neck.

"You're even prettier as a swan," he said. Signe gave him her intelligent stare and sailed away.

13

He didn't even notice how the thorns and branches in the maze of bushes tore at him. All he could think about was returning to Larkey. And then he was there, in the back room. He heard the light snoring of the two women and tiptoed through the dining room and into the kitchen, which was still dark. He banged into one of the chairs and a cat mewed and he realized all four cats were asleep together on one of the tables.

In the half-light of the dismally cold streets he walked for several blocks until he found a taxi.

Fulcho was sound asleep on the couch and Norman sat down next to him and patted him on the head.

"Mrrrrr," he said without opening his eyes.

"Fulcho—Fuoco—do you know your name almost means 'fire' in Italian?" The cat began to purr. "Fulcho, tonight I saw a cat who turned into a swan. She was beautiful. Like Larkey, like you."

He put Fulcho on his shoulder while he pulled the bed out of the couch, then laid him tenderly down on the pillow. Fulcho sat up grouchily and groomed himself for a few minutes, then curled up on the same spot on which Norman had placed him while Norman undressed in the dark.

"It's morning, Fulcho, but I won't open the blinds, so we'll never know."

He was asleep instantly, possessed by dreams of Larkey smiling, making love to him. And the memory of a beautiful black swan whose head he had patted and a little crone who had been Cinderella for a night.

His head was clanging. Fulcho was mewing at him.

"What?" he said, and realized it was the telephone.

"Norman, it's Sharon. Are you all right?"

"Oh, yes, what time is it, Sharon?"

"That's the second time you've asked me that since I know you. I liked the first time better. It's nine thirty. I'm sorry I woke you, but I was worried. I called you until one o'clock this morning. I was so worried about your going to your aunts' last night."

"Why?"

"I don't know. Premonition, maybe. I finally gave up and had nightmares all night about that place."

Norman turned the lamp on. If she has nightmares without ever having seen the place, he thought . . .

"What are you doing today, Norman?"

"Well, I have to go downtown and do my martyr chores." And I have a date at noon in my fantasy world, he thought.

"Do you think we can get together— Oh, there I go again."

"I'd rather let you know later—or tomorrow, Sharon. I don't know how long I'll have to stay there. I'm sorry, Sharon, I don't mean to keep doing this."

"That's O.K. I even called Uncle Fred late last night when I couldn't reach you. He said he wouldn't dream of telling me anything you discussed, just that he hoped you wouldn't go down there much longer. Are you leaving soon?"

"Soon. Yes." He yawned. "I have to take a shower and— Oh, my God!"

"Norman! What's the matter?"

"Oh, my God."

"Norman? What happened?"

"It's nothing, nothing. I . . . uh . . . don't worry about it. I'm very melodramatic in the morning. I have to go now, Sharon. Thank you for calling. Goodbye."

"Oh, my God," he continued saying to himself as he looked down. The insides of his thighs were caked with dried blood.

14

He continued staring. No more imaginings, no more fantasy. She was real. It was all real. He began to shake, and Fulcho walked over to him and mewed softly. He patted the cat and stared at him, then put his pillow over his face and screamed into it.

He felt faint. He went to the refrigerator, opened a bottle of champagne and drank it all down in a water glass. Then he reached into the cigarette box and removed the stickpin. Would there be a trace, a thread, from Larkey's dress? He turned it over. On the back, where the pin was welded to the jewel setting, was painted a tiny peony. He shuddered. Did he really need this extra proof?

He telephoned Fred, who picked up on the first ring. "You chose a good time, Norman. I'm just between loonies. What's happening?"

Norman spat out every detail, talking so quickly that his words became jumbled. Several times Fred had to ask him to stop and start again.

When he was all finished, Fred said, "Just listen to me, Norman. See whether you might have cut yourself on something during the night."

"Fred, I'm not blind. I have no cuts or bruises, and I'll tell you something else. I know how my body feels after making love and that's how it felt last night. And, please, no lectures about nocturnal emissions. It happened, Fred, it really happened. And now they're going to have to tell me the truth."

Fred was silent. "Norman, I'm fighting for some rational explanation and hoping at the same time that there isn't one. You'd make a hell of a chapter in my book. I don't know what to tell you. Just take care of yourself and call me again if you need— Just call me. Call me later."

Norman forced himself into the shower and, feeling as if he was pouring acid over himself, washed off the blood as Larkey's words came back: "This I have given you."

By the time he was dressed he was staggering, and he realized that drinking an entire bottle of champagne in the morning wasn't the smartest thing in the world to do.

He telephoned Amy.

"Oh, Norman, I have terrible news," she said. "So terrible."

"Is Aunt Elizabeth— Did something happen to Aunt Elizabeth?"

"No, nothing like that." Was she going to tell him something now?

"Speak up!" he heard Elizabeth shout. "I can't hear a word you're saying!"

"What's the terrible news, Aunt Amy?"

"What? Oh. Ronnie and Freddie were robbed."

"Who?"

"Ronnie and Freddie. You know, our neighbors who get us our—the things we smoke. They were mugged during the night. They have bruises and cuts and Ronnie says if that knife had been an inch closer to him it would have gone right through his heart. Oh, Norman, we're so scared. They're going to come back, I know it. Next time it'll be us. I'm so afraid. Norman, please hurry down here." But she wasn't afraid of anything that could happen to her in another world.

"Should I call the police, Aunt Amy?"

"Police? I think they—"

"No police!" Elizabeth shouted.

"Norman," Amy pleaded, "just come down here. Darling, we haven't had breakfast yet, so on your way could you pick up a milk and a package of instant tacos? She has them downstairs."

Norman tried to keep steady as he walked through the streets, but it wasn't the champagne that made him feel the way he did. He was amazed at the blueness of the sky, the brightness of clothing on people, the contrasting colors of cars. He noticed tops of buildings and street signs for the first time. This is what you've done for me, Larkey, he thought.

His reverie ended at Berkenblitt's Bargains.

"Why, good morning, Norman," Natalie said through pursed lips. "Did you have a pleasant night?"

He nodded.

"Has Signe been found?"

He shook his head.

"A shame," she said. "She was a beauty. Too little beauty in the world, if you know what I mean." She gave him her conspiratorial smile and raised an eyebrow. "They want these tacos heated?"

"I guess."

"They certainly eat the funniest foods," she said, staring at him. "At least if you go by their orders to me. You never know." She gave him her sidelong glance. "Perhaps they're taking some of their meals someplace else. Could that be it?"

He shrugged.

"You don't talk much, do you? Maybe the missing cat's got your tongue." Her strange "hmm, hmm, hmm" accompanied him out of the store.

And turned into uproarious laughter in the building, which he heard as soon as he hit the first landing. When he walked into the kitchen, facing him were Elizabeth, in the rocking chair, holding a marijuana joint and breathing in hard; Amy, trying to control her laughter; and two young men in their early twenties who were a medley of long blond hair, denim, Band-aids and beards.

"Ronnie and Freddie," Elizabeth said grandly, "I would like to introduce you to Norman." Then she and Amy burst out laughing again. Norman thought, My life has turned upside down and they're laughing their heads off.

The boys shook hands with him.

The one who was Freddie said, "Your aunts have been telling us great things about you. Want a drag?"

Norman shook his head.

"How did you get out of bed?" Norman asked Elizabeth.

She smiled. "The boys helped me. But we still won't let Freddie have his way."

Norman's heart began to pound. "What won't you let him do?"

Freddie answered. "Oh, I'm taking my master's in film and I wanted to use the ladies in a two-reeler I'm doing for my final."

Elizabeth laughed again. "I don't think the world of cinema is ready for us yet." Then she winked at Ronnie. "Young man, I may be a dinosaur to you, but duels have been fought over the kind of look you're giving me now."

Freddie shook his head and smiled at Norman. "Can you see why I'd like to use them in a film? These aunts of yours are outrageous."

Elizabeth laughed. "You don't know the half, son."

Norman put his hands over his ears.

"We may be a little spaced," said Freddie, "but we've been through a lot. I thought at one point during the night that I was down for the count. He chipped one of my teeth." He pointed to the tooth and Norman nodded.

"They got our TV, my midget Sony, all our Stones albums, Freddie's college ring, my microscope, eighty-three dollars in cash, four film cans of grass and my good suede jacket," Ronnie said.

"How did they get in?" Norman asked.

"They knocked. They must know this building. They gave a certain kind of signal on the door and we thought it was my girl friend coming to spend the night."

Elizabeth laughed again. "Serves you right." Then she developed a coughing fit.

Freddie rushed over to her. "Is there anything I can get for you, Duchess?" he asked.

"No," she said when she'd calmed down. "Too much laughing always does it to me. I should know better. But I can't help it, can I, Amy?"

"No, she can't," said Amy seriously.

"Well, we'd better leave," said Ronnie.

"I'll walk you out," Norman said.

In the hallway Ronnie said, "Want to see our place?"

"No, thanks." *I've seen it.*

"Hey," said Freddie, "those are good ladies in there." He smiled. "They're the only almost-royalty we've ever met. Look, if you ever need some help with them, just call us any time, O.K.? We're not particular about when we wake up. And it's kind of fun for us going in there. We call it Liz'n' Amy's antique store."

They disappeared into their apartment.

Norman locked the door behind him.

"That's a good boy," said Elizabeth. "We're so disturbed about that robbery. They could easily break in and kill us too."

"Did you have a pleasant night, Aunt Elizabeth?" Norman asked, trying to keep his voice steady.

"I haven't had a good night in eight years. Why?"

He removed his coat and hung it on a finial of one of the clocks.

"Because, Aunt Elizabeth, I want to talk to you—seriously."

Amy's eyes were frightened. She reached into her pocket, took out her little ball and began to squeeze it rapidly.

"Stop it, Aunt Amy."

She put the ball back into her pocket, picked up the feather duster and headed for the dining room.

"Don't leave, Aunt Amy. I want you to hear this too."

"I have to clean this place. It's so untidy."

"Sit down, Aunt Amy," he said menacingly.

Her lip began to quiver and she moved one of the broken chairs next to the rocker, sat down and put her head on her sister's shoulder.

"I came back here last night after you two went to sleep.

Yes, I walked into this apartment, using the key I had made. I went into that back room. Nothing fell on my head. I just walked through the bushes and there I was."

"Are you starting—" Elizabeth said imperiously.

"Shut up, Aunt Elizabeth, I'm not finished."

"I don't like the way you're talking," she said indignantly.

"You don't like the way I'm talking? Well, I don't like a lot of things around here myself," he said. "To continue. I spent the whole evening there, at a dance in a ballroom with a stained-glass roof. At the dance were Lorenzo Ferromonte, you two, my mother, Larkey and Monk Abruzzi. You were wearing a green silky dress, Aunt Elizabeth, and you were wearing yellow, Aunt Amy. Larkey wore a red dress, on which was the diamond stickpin you gave me the other night. She said she was going to give it to you for Grandpa Simon." He paused and stared at each of them. "Pearlie Gish was at the dance too. Do you still want to tell me I'm imagining things?"

"You could have found out a lot of these facts from other places," Elizabeth said quickly.

"O.K., Aunt Elizabeth. I hope this won't shock you, and God forgive me for saying it. Larkey and I made love last night in her all-white room in the Ferromonte house. She was a virgin. And I had blood on me this morning."

Elizabeth closed her eyes and lowered her head.

"Well, my dear aunts," he said through gritted teeth, "do you want more information?"

Elizabeth started to shake and folded her arms across her chest to steady herself. For the first time in her life she sounded defeated.

"It's all over, Amy," she muttered half audibly. "All over." She began to sob. "Oh, God, haven't we given up enough?" Then she turned to Norman, her face frightened, and let out a long sigh.

"Yes, Norman, we were all there. I don't know how it happened. The first time you were there was also the first time we were there."

He raised an eyebrow.

"No, I'm telling the truth, may God strike me dead. Until Wednesday night it was all a memory. Oh, we'd been in that back room before." She nodded toward the door. "But it never took us to the Ferromonte house. For years, you see"—she smiled, her face softening and giving back a hint of the great beauty once contained on it—"we've been going in there and visiting our house on Fifth Avenue. Lots of times we saw you as a little boy. Just the other day we were playing with you. Oh, how you laughed. Remember when you said you heard music and dancing? We were there, in the house on Fifth Avenue. We've been spending most of our time there, you see."

Norman blinked. "That first day I came here I heard 'How Do You Do, My Partner?' and a baby laughing. That was *me*, wasn't it?"

She nodded.

He shook his head. "You just walked into the room and went back in time. Didn't you ever question it?"

"Why? You question bad things, not good ones."

Something nagged at him and he remembered. "Natalie was never at the real house uptown, was she?"

Elizabeth sighed deeply again. "We might as well tell you everything. The day of your mother's funeral we stopped in the store and, well, Natalie asked us whether we wanted to take in a homeless kitten. She seemed to want to be kind, and she said taking care of the animal might keep our minds off our loss. We were so grief-stricken we agreed. And since that afternoon we've been going back to the old house.

"At first we thought we'd gone crazy. Then we found proof —oh, so many kinds of proof—and we decided to thank Natalie for giving us Signe, for giving us our lives back, and to invite her to come there with us. Well, she behaved horribly. She—" Elizabeth looked down at the floor.

"What did she do?" Norman asked.

"I'd rather not discuss it."

"You'd better tell me," he demanded.

"She— Oh, Amy, you tell him."

Amy's frightened eyes stared at him. When she finally spoke she sounded like a child reciting a nursery rhyme. "She seduced Daddy. Less than two hours after we invited her into the garden, Elizabeth and I found her with him. It was the most shocking, awful sight we've ever seen."

"Now you know why we never invited her back," Elizabeth said. "For years she's been tormenting us, asking us. We've given her every excuse under the sun."

"You mean, after what she did, she still asked you to take her there?" he asked. Now all of Natalie's strange behavior fell into place.

"We never acknowledged that we saw her with Daddy," Elizabeth sobbed.

"Why? Aunt Elizabeth, you of all people. Why didn't you confront her with what she is? Why do you continue associating with her at all? There are other grocery stores around here."

Amy's wailing began again.

"Hush, Amy, child, you'll be all right," said Elizabeth softly. "Don't you understand, Norman? We're deathly afraid of her. We're afraid we'll be punished and that the back room will be taken away from us if we stop buying from her. Norman, do you think we enjoy living in this squalor? Don't you remember the way we used to live?" She lowered her voice. "Do you know the Greek word 'hubris'? Too much pride. Being as we were was too high and mighty for people, and we thought if we totally reduced our circumstances, maybe we'd earn the right. That's one of the reasons we gave up the rest of the apartment."

"I don't understand you," Norman said. "Couldn't you have lived a spartan existence in a larger place?"

"No," she said. "Signe wouldn't have it."

"What?"

"Norman, *she* selected that back room, and it was only in that room that we could go back to the old house. One day we tried to take her into my bedroom—you remember where it used to be—and she screamed and cried so, we thought she'd gone beserk. And every time we tried to take her anywhere beyond that room she acted the same way, and then we couldn't go back to our old house for days. It was Signe's way of telling us we had to give up the rest of the apartment."

Norman shook his head and hit the side of the grandfather clock against which he'd been leaning, and the chimes went off.

"They haven't worked in years," Amy said.

"I don't believe what you're saying," he said. "A cat was responsible for all this. I don't understand."

"Don't you see? It became very clear to us that the more we give up in this world, the more time we could spend in the back room. You see what's happened to everything here, all ruined, smashed."

"Did you—"

Elizabeth nodded. "Yes, we did it. We purposely ruined it all. My beautiful bed. Do you know the headboard was painted by Joshua Reynolds? Haven't you noticed? We've smeared black paint all over it."

"Why couldn't you just get rid of the furniture?"

She sobbed. "We were afraid. You can't imagine what Signe put us through after I gave Charles the Tiffany lamp. One day we tried to give away that Chippendale desk and she attacked us! You wouldn't believe the strength of that little animal. So we just kept it all. And that's the way we've lived for eight years. Norman, is it like us to drink cheap wines, or to spend our days eating pizza and vulgar candy? We may be a little senile, but we still have our proper ways. We've been eating most of our meals at our real house uptown."

Norman gasped. He pressed his hands against the sides of his head. And he realized the clock was still chiming. "Doesn't this ever shut off?" he shouted. "It must be three hundred o'clock by now!" He smashed his fist against it and heard the rapid spinning of wires and then silence. Amy laughed, then covered her mouth.

"Norman, dear," Elizabeth continued, "we're even afraid of

laughing too much. Have you noticed the coughing fits we develop almost every time we laugh? Laughter means happiness and we can't have too much happiness here, or it will take longer. Maybe we'll never get there at all." Now she began to cry again.

"Please, Aunt Elizabeth, Aunt Amy."

"Oh, I'm so scared," Amy sobbed.

"Why did you keep Signe locked up?"

Elizabeth wiped her eyes. "Except for those times in the beginning when she attacked us, until we complied with her wishes, she was a perfectly normal cat."

"A normal cat!" he shouted. "A normal cat who has the power to take you back forty-five years?"

"Hush, Norman, let me finish. Difficult as it may be to believe, she was a normal, loving cat. Until one day a couple of years ago, the day Natalie gave us some turkey to give to her. We knew it was one of her ploys to get into our good graces, so we'd invite her. Well, I don't know what possessed us."

She looked at Amy. "Maybe Natalie exerted some kind of power over us, but Amy and I suddenly got very gluttonous and ate the turkey ourselves. Well, it was as though Signe knew it, and she leaped up onto the table and attacked us and stayed outside the back room and stalked us. Every time we came near her she scratched us viciously. That bittie thing was like a tiger. And we knew we would never get into that back room again unless she was kept locked up. So we—I—put gloves on and grabbed her and, while Amy held the door open, we threw her into the bathroom, where we kept her until we had the screen door made for the pantry."

This is really happening, he told himself. "You know, I think Signe is now a swan," he said.

Elizabeth shivered and covered her eyes. "We know."

"Why did you name her Signe, Aunt Elizabeth?"

"We didn't. That was her name when Natalie gave her to us. Oh, Norman, it's been so long and so painful."

"And why couldn't you tell all this to me before now?" he asked. "Instead of all your games and innuendos."

"We thought we couldn't trust you," Elizabeth said.

"Me? You couldn't trust me? Why?"

"Hush, Norman. No need for temper now. After we made that first visit to the Ferromonte garden Tuesday night we were terrified. We sat up all night trying to figure it out, but decided to wait and see. Then, just before you got here Wednesday, I went into the room by myself and I was back at our house on Fifth Avenue, but nobody was there. It was then I knew you had some kind of power and I decided we were going to have it out with you, but I had to stall for time to plot my strategy."

He laughed. "Strategy?"

"Yes, Norman, strategy. Remember Wednesday evening when I sent you for the wine and said I was going to tell you something important when you returned? While you were out we paid our second visit to Renzo's house and I got really frightened. I was afraid if we told you about it that something terrible would happen to us."

"We were so shocked, Norman," Amy said. "We were never there before. You see—"

"Why don't you let me finish?" Elizabeth commanded.

"Let *me* talk!" pleaded Amy. "She never lets me say a word!"

"Very well, love, you wanted the floor," said Elizabeth. "It's all yours."

"Norman," said Amy, "we were so afraid of what happened and we knew it was because of you. We couldn't figure it out. We thought you might be working for the C.I.A. or the Mafia and were going to turn us in."

"C.I.A. *or* the Mafia? I don't think those organizations, similar as they may be, specialize in magic," he said. "What made you think of them?"

"Well, Norman, you have very irregular working hours, and yesterday afternoon when Pearlie tried to call you in the office—we didn't tell you this—she was told employees are not allowed to accept telephone calls. Well, that sounded pretty odd."

Norman yelped, fell into a chair and thought he would never stop laughing. Two old ladies playing with magic, but underneath, still two frightened old ladies. When he was able to control himself he looked at Elizabeth, then at Amy. "But I'm your nephew, your only flesh and blood, with the exception of my wonderful brother in California. How could you possibly think I would harm you?"

"We didn't know, Norman, darling," Elizabeth said. "And we were so worried. Do you know what it did to me—how it hurt my heart—to have to hit you on the head?"

"You hit me on the head?"

Elizabeth nodded. "God forgive me, Norman. Both times. Not with a candlestick, though." She shook her head sadly.

"With what?" he asked.

She looked at the floor and bit her lip. "A can of cat food. I couldn't hold anything heavier. Oh, Norman, as long as I live I'll regret doing that to my precious nephew. I would rather have done it to myself."

The telephone rang. Norman snapped up the receiver.

"Hello, is this Norman?" came the creaky little voice.

"Yes."

"This is Miss Gish from upstairs—Pearlie. How are your aunts today?"

"They're fine."

"May I speak to them?"

"I'm sorry, Pearlie, they're napping now. Can I give them a message?"

"No, just tell them . . . tell them I have a wonderful story about a dream I had last night. You were in it too, Norman. Tell them, and they can call me later."

He hung up and tried to control his voice. "That was Pearlie."

Now he stared at Elizabeth. "How did she get to the ball last night?" Both women were silent. "Answer me. How did she get there?"

"We don't know, Norman," Elizabeth cried. "We don't understand anything any more. Please don't shout. We never told her a word about that back room. We thought you brought her in with you."

"I? Why should I?" He wondered. Was he exerting some kind of control? They had said they were never there before he went there, and he was never there before he extended a kindness to a black cat with white furrows on her brow. A kindness. Hadn't he thought, just the other day, that Pearlie was kind to his aunts? And why had Signe chosen that particular room in which to work her magic, that room that was always his favorite as a child? No, none of this made any sense.

"Aunt Elizabeth, I have a really snobbish question. How did you ever get friendly with Pearlie . . . and the boys next door?"

Elizabeth nodded. "The same reason we drink cheap wines, Norman. But I'll tell you something we've learned, some of the plainest people in the world are also the loveliest. Pearlie has been as kind to us as though she were a member of our own family. And the boys, they've run errands for us, and they give us that happy weed, and, you know something? They're beautiful people. When we were young we never looked below the surface. We never had to. I was always very big on causes, so long as I never had to deal directly with people. Ah, it's a little late to get philosophical." She looked at Norman and in a small voice asked, "What are you going to do to us now?"

"Nothing. You don't have to worry, Aunt Elizabeth. I want to find out more about this."

"You mustn't question too closely," Elizabeth said, then began to cry. "Oh, I'm so afraid it will all disappear."

"It won't disappear," he said. "It's funny, isn't it, that the door was jammed shut so tight that first time I touched it. Like a wind or something was keeping it sealed. And it only opened after I gave the turkey to Signe. Jesus Christ!"

"Please don't take the name of the Lord in vain in addition to everything else," Elizabeth said nervously.

The telephone rang again. Norman picked up the receiver. "Hello." He heard a click and he hung up.

"Who was it?" Elizabeth asked.

"Nobody. Click-off."

"It must be Natalie," Amy said. "She hasn't stopped calling us since we got the phone put in."

"Now do you know why we didn't want it, Norman?" Elizabeth asked. "She's been calling and teasing us and asking us when we're going to invite her again. It's gotten so we're afraid to pick up the receiver. Oh, Norman, she's a witch! How did she know we had a telephone?"

Norman smiled. "She probably saw the installation man coming into the building. Word seems to travel fast around here." He laughed. "Hey, Aunt Elizabeth, what ever happened to the peonies I brought you?"

Elizabeth looked down. "We took them with us to the back room. They were too pretty to be here. They're somewhere in the garden of our house on Fifth Avenue now."

He shook his head again. "Well, I don't know about the house on Fifth Avenue, but I have an appointment with Larkey as soon as Monk leaves for Palermo."

"I thought he left," Elizabeth said.

"I have later information."

Elizabeth gasped. "Of course, of course, Norman. You have *all* the information now, don't you? Oh, Norman!" She began to cry again. "Don't be cruel to your old aunts, please."

"Cruel? Why should I?"

"Will you let us go with you today?" Amy asked plaintively.

"I wouldn't think of going without you." He smiled, and Elizabeth's sobs ended. "Just tell me something, one thing. What happened to Larkey after she left the Ferromonte house to marry Monk?"

"I don't know," Elizabeth said.

He knocked a chair over. "Do you want to go back with me or don't you?" he shouted.

"I mean it," she squealed. "I don't know. Am I lying, Amy?"

"She went to Rome that Monday afternoon and that was the last time we saw her, when she gave the diamond pin to Elizabeth."

Elizabeth started to cry again. "Why are you being so harsh

with us, Norman? We were always so good to you when you were a baby. You should have seen us with you last week. So help me God, we never heard another thing about Larkey. It isn't as though we didn't ask. But if anybody knew something it wasn't being told to us. To this day we don't have a single clue as to what happened to her."

"What about Monk? He was pretty well known in Italy at the time."

"He either disappeared without a trace or everybody was keeping secrets from us."

"Don't think we haven't wondered all these years," said Amy. "We've asked ourselves a thousand times what could have happened to Larkey. She was such a joy. Elizabeth, remember those teeny buttons she used to paint? What ever became of them?"

Elizabeth didn't answer.

"She was wearing them just the other day," Norman said quietly.

"No," said Amy, "that's not what I mean. We had some, we used to have some here, in this house." She looked at him, then broke into a smile, her eyes shining, and exclaimed, "Oh, Norman, aren't we beautiful when we go there? What do you think of your mother? That's what we mean when we tell you what the Gould sisters were in those days. Such lovely days."

"You two are pretty good actresses," Norman said.

"All our lives we've had to be actresses," Elizabeth said bitterly.

"That's not what I mean. In all these visits I've made to that place, you and Amy never once even hinted that you knew who I really was."

"But, Norman," said Amy, "when we're there, we *don't* know who you are. It's only when we come back."

"Why do you come back?"

"What?" Elizabeth moaned, covering her eyes.

"Why do you come back?"

"Why do you think, Norman? It's always the same. We hear

the screaming cats, that unbearable sound, and the only way to make it stop is to come back. We don't know what it is. Maybe we haven't sacrificed enough." Now she sobbed. "You'd think we'd given up everything and that finally . . . What do we have in this world that we still have to keep coming back here?"

"Besides," Amy said, "who would feed our cats if we never came back?"

Elizabeth's sobbing stopped, and the imperious voice returned in full force. "Oh, will you listen to her? Who would feed our cats. Can you see what I've had to contend with all these years? I yearn for paradise and she worries about feeding cats. Oh, Lord, I'm in such pain. I've got to lie down."

Norman looked at his watch. "It's twelve thirty-five. There's no time difference there, though I don't know why I expect anything to have a reason any more. It's not necessary for you to lie down, Aunt Elizabeth. We're going there now."

Elizabeth looked at Norman with frightened eyes. "Oh, Norman, I'm afraid. I'm really afraid."

"Of what?"

"I'm afraid Natalie is going to follow us."

"That's ridiculous. How can she follow us?"

"How, Norman? You need to ask how? She gave us Signe and now Signe is there. Maybe she's going to go there to get her back." She started to sob.

"There's nothing to worry about, Aunt Elizabeth," he said. "If Natalie had some special powers, she wouldn't need an invitation to get in there. Hasn't that occurred to you? Besides"—his voice sounded odd to him— "I wouldn't let her in."

Both old ladies smiled at him.

"That's our Norman!" Amy exclaimed. "The first man in our lives since Daddy who's willing to protect us."

Norman smiled. He looked at the two frail women, so small and helpless, waiting for him to guide them into their other world, and he thought, They're like the Munchkins from Munchkinland. And I'm the goddamn Wizard of Oz.

15

Amy limped quickly toward the dining room, and Norman helped Elizabeth out of the rocker in painful steps and slowly led her to the back room.

"Watch those branches!" Elizabeth shouted. "They'll scratch your face up."

They were there, but when Norman got through, Elizabeth and Amy came walking toward him from Appia Antica.

"Norman, oh, there you are!" Elizabeth shouted in English.

"We have such exciting news for you!" Amy exclaimed.

Elizabeth put her silken-gloved hand over Amy's mouth. "*Silencio*, my dear. It's my news and I'll tell it. Norman, Lorenzo Ferromonte has asked me to marry him!"

Norman smiled. He couldn't take his eyes off these two beautiful women, the older one in a long sky-blue garden dress, the other in a similar pink outfit, both with those lovely eyes and hair.

"I envy him," Norman said, "but it must have been a difficult choice. You are all so beautiful."

Amy laughed, but Elizabeth said haughtily, "Thank you, Norman. But perhaps Renzo sees more than beauty."

"I think there's a subtle insult there," Amy mused, then smiled at Norman. "My older sister wanted to be the first lady Prime Minister of England." She turned to Elizabeth. "But I guess now you'll want to be the first lady President of Italy?"

"We'll see which offer comes in first." Elizabeth laughed.

"And what do you want to be, Amy?" Norman asked.

"Just somebody's loving wife." Amy smiled. "I've never had great ambitions. Daddy says I'm too submissive, but that's the way I like to be."

"And how about your sister Maria?" Norman asked.

"Maria will probably go on the stage, unless she dies of acute champagne poisoning first," Elizabeth said.

Norman heard the noise of a motor on the road.

"That must be the car come to pick up Monk," Amy said.

Norman backed away. "Where is Monk?" he asked.

"Out on the road," Elizabeth answered, "saying goodbye to Larkey. I must say, Norman, you and Larkey are living dangerously."

Norman walked to the wall separating the estate from Appia Antica and peered around a corner. A chauffered white Duesenberg idled there, against which stood Monk Abruzzi, his arms around Larkey.

"You have never been more beautiful, Larkey," Norman heard Monk say. "Two more days . . ." Then his voice got steely. "Just remember what I have told you."

She said something, too softly for Norman to make out, and Monk got into the car and was driven off.

Larkey stood there for a while, her back to Norman, then turned toward the estate, tears streaming down her face, and walked right past him.

"Larkey," he said, grabbing her arm.

"Oh, Norman." She leaned against him and wiped her eyes. Her hair smelled of jasmine. "I am so glad you came back."

He kissed her.

"It might be a good idea for you two to play out your drama back in the house," Elizabeth said, smiling. "Monk may just decide to come back for something."

"It's lunchtime anyway," Amy said. "Where's Maria?"

"Probably making gigantic inroads on the wine cellar," Elizabeth said dryly.

The four of them walked toward the house. As they approached the pond, Signe sailed to the edge. Norman led Larkey up to her and Signe, as she had done the night before, put her head against Norman's chest and her beak under his arm.

"Look at the swan trying to kiss Norman!" Amy exclaimed.

Larkey smiled at Signe. "I do not blame you, little swan."

Signe looked up at Norman and swam away.

"I've never seen a swan do anything like that," Amy said.

"Since when are you an expert on swans?" Elizabeth asked.

Norman was amazed at the stillness of the air. Not a bird call, not even the buzzing of insects.

When they got to the house, Larkey said, "Norman and I will join you shortly."

Elizabeth raised an eyebrow but said nothing.

"We're lunching out at the fountain today," Amy said.

Larkey led him up to her room, locked the door behind them and kissed him.

Norman looked toward the bed. "What did you do with the cover?"

She laughed. "I promised an ungodly bribe to one of the maids to take care of it. Now we needn't worry about that happening again."

"It is even better the second time," she whispered as they lay close together. "It is better—and yet it will never be the same. The wild, crazy discovery of the first time can never happen twice. But now I have the joy of knowing that the pleasure will come again and again, and with more ecstasy each time."

He tried to blot out the thought of Monk taking that pleasure from her.

"Larkey, how do you know so much?"

"I didn't know much at all until the day I saw you in the garden. Norman, have you given yourself to many women before me?"

He stared at her. "Not really. I've never given myself to anybody but you."

"Oh, Norman, I love you so. But if we don't get down to lunch soon they will surely be gossiping about us."

"I think they all know."

"Of course they all know, my darling. I was joking. I think I shall forevermore be known as the *meretrice* of the Ferromonte estate."

The luncheon crowd at the fountain was fairly high on champagne by the time they got there. Seated around the fountain, besides the Gould girls and Renzo, were two of his friends who had been invited to escort Amy and Maria for the day.

Elizabeth held the floor. "Well, does everybody give up?"

They all nodded.

"A.F.F.—Archduke Franz Ferdinand! What could have been more obvious!" Elizabeth exclaimed. Amy, Maria and Renzo applauded.

One of the young men asked, "Who is he?"

"Who *is* he?" Elizabeth laughed. "Gino, go back to your history books. It was only because of his assassination that the Great War started—a mere fourteen years ago! Where were you fourteen years ago, in a cocoon?"

Maria spotted Norman and Larkey. "Have a good siesta?" she asked.

Larkey blushed and Elizabeth shot Maria a dirty look, then shrugged and joined in the laughter.

"Won't you have some recently crushed French grapes to celebrate my impending marriage?" Renzo asked Norman in English.

"It is only *impending* upon how father feels about it," Elizabeth joked.

"Surely," said Gino, "your father cannot object to your living in a palace like this."

"We don't exactly live in a gardener's cottage at the moment," Elizabeth said.

"You know, Renzo," Amy said, "you should be honored. This is the fortieth marriage proposal Elizabeth has received."

"Forty-first," Elizabeth said. "Sultan Zahir proposed twice."

Amy laughed. "He wanted to make Elizabeth his number one wife. She wanted to be wives one through six."

Elizabeth said dryly, "He couldn't conceive of such a thing, if you'll pardon the double entendre."

Renzo took Elizabeth's hand. "Elizabeth, do you really mean that if your father is against our marriage you will give in to his wishes?"

Elizabeth patted Renzo's hand. "I always comply with my father's wishes," she said, then smiled. "But my father also knows enough to comply with mine."

"He's like the rest of the world," Maria mumbled.

"Quiet, you little drunk," said Elizabeth.

Larkey clinked her glass lightly against Norman's. "To us, forever," she said. "Forever will be two days."

"Larkey," he whispered, "are you sure we should be here? Monk has informants."

"If one of them is his spy, it is now too late, isn't it?" she said, smiling.

They were on the same bench he'd sat on two million years ago last night, and butlers distributed a banquet of cold courses.

"Zabaglione," Norman said thoughtfully as the waiter handed them dessert.

"Are you familiar with this dish in the United States?" Larkey asked.

He nodded.

Gino and his friend were fussing over Elizabeth, who had just lit a cigarette.

"In Rome women who smoke are considered . . . well . . ." laughed Gino.

"They're considered the same in London." Amy giggled. "But Elizabeth doesn't care. She's one of the 'new' women. And you should hear the way she swears sometimes. Shocks our whole family."

Elizabeth ignored her sister. "Would Signor Ferromonte consider taking us to the beach today?"

"Wonderful idea!" Renzo replied. "Everybody interested?

Good. Why don't we get our bathing clothes and meet at the garage at three thirty?"

"May I drive the first car?" Elizabeth asked.

Renzo smiled indulgently. "You, my dear?"

Elizabeth raised an eyebrow. "Don't you 'my dear' me, Renzo," she said indignantly. "If you expect to spend a lifetime with me you'd better get used to some facts, one of which is that I can drive a car better than any man."

"Wait till you hear the rest of the facts, Renzo," Maria said.

Elizabeth gave her sister a smoldering look. "Before I'm finished in this world, I'll see to it that divorce laws are rewritten to include sisters."

"So long as they exclude Italian husbands," Renzo said.

Elizabeth smiled and stroked his cheek.

Larkey walked over to Renzo and spoke to him privately, then returned to Norman. "I asked Renzo to excuse us from the beach excursion. He is going to lend us one of the cars to use as we please." She squeezed his hand. "Today I will show you Rome. Can you drive a car?"

"Probably not as well as Aunt Elizabeth."

"*Aunt* Elizabeth!" Larkey laughed and impulsively kissed him. "Let's go to the garage." Norman wondered whether he could drive a 1928 car and also what he would do if he were stopped by a policeman.

They were led to a gleaming black Italian coupe, and for the first time in his life he saw a rumble seat.

He glanced at the dashboard, clutch and shift and thanked God he had learned to drive on an Army jeep.

"I think you'll have to direct me, Larkey."

"You mean you don't know your way into the city?"

"I have a very poor sense of direction."

"I hardly think so," she said, smiling intimately, and they both laughed.

He squinted, because the sun was blazing into his eyes through the windshield. "I wonder whether they have sunglasses yet?"

"Why do you say it in such an odd way?" She reached into the glove compartment and extracted a small pair of rimless round tinted glasses. Same as 1973, he thought, and started the car.

"It is straight down Appia Antica into town," Larkey said.

Town, he thought. The Eternal City is town to her.

"Larkey, could you point out the sights as we come to them?"

"Norman, you act as though you've sprung from another planet."

"I've never been to Rome before. I came here from the South."

In a few moments they passed the tomb of Cecelia Metella and, beyond that, several other tombs. All along the way the road was lined with statues.

They were now on a wider road. "There, over there on the left, the Baths of Caracalla," she said. They drove on silently, then suddenly Norman looked ahead of him, gasped and almost lost control of the car.

"That's the Colosseum!" he exclaimed.

"I know that, Norman."

"But I didn't— I mean, I never saw it before."

"I'm sorry for talking to you like that, Norman dear, but, you see, we Romans are used to our sights. Over on the left is even better. The Forum. I must take you there, but first keep going in this direction and I shall tell you where to turn."

He tried to contain the wild excitement he felt, driving through this other world.

"Ahead of you," she said, "is part of the old wall of Rome."

"I've never seen anything like this in my life."

"You do not have beautiful sights in New York?"

Sure, he thought. Subways, graffiti, muggings, traffic jams, and whole floorsful of people waiting for elevators to take them to lunch at twelve noon exactly.

"Yes, we certainly have some sights in New York."

"I should love to visit there someday."

"Maybe you will, Larkey."

They drove into a park that was so spectacularly beautiful

that Norman thought it must be a re-creation of the Garden of Eden. Past hundreds of marble busts, flowers, trees, cavorting children, a lake, and then they parked under a tree.

"The Borghese Gardens," she said, "and now I shall take you to the Gallery."

Up the steps of a magnificent building and into the building they went. Norman marveled at its beauty.

"Does this remind you of Renzo's house?" Larkey asked.

"I was just thinking that."

"It was once the home of the Borghese family and, I am told, was designed by the same man and built in the same year. Do you not have wonderful galleries and museums in New York?"

"Yes, but they don't have marble floors and pictures on the ceiling. Larkey, do you sometimes dream that your paintings—your little flowers and faces—will be in a gallery?"

She laughed. "My painting is about as important as my life and will be remembered as much." She said this with a total absence of self-pity, and Norman took her hand and kissed it.

They wandered through the galleries until Norman stared ahead at something and stopped.

"That reclining figure, is she real?"

Larkey laughed. "You mean Pauline?"

"Who?"

"Pauline Borghese. Everybody who comes here thinks she is real."

They approached the gleaming white marble statue and he stared at its exquisite lines.

"Larkey, she looks like you."

"You think my body is that nice?"

"Don't you know by now?"

A guard came into the room and told them the Gallery was closing for the day.

Larkey took his hand. "Wait, let us not go yet." She led him into another room, in which hung heavy draperies. "Let us hide behind them."

"Why?"

"You shall see."

They slipped behind the thick fabric, Larkey holding his hand tight.

"Now we must stand very still until they have all gone."

"Are you going to tell me why?"

"I want for us to be all alone in this building. For all of my life, since I first entered here, I have wanted to be here alone. It is only today I have felt like sharing it."

Norman coughed. "If the guards don't leave soon, we may be sharing a grave."

She giggled. And they waited, minute after minute.

"We needn't stand side by side," she said and leaned against his chest. He kissed her.

"I guess if you have to suffocate this isn't a bad way to go," he said.

She covered his mouth. "Let us listen." Then she slipped out from behind the drapery. "All right, Norman, it is still now."

Hand in hand, they walked through all the silent rooms, finishing in front of Pauline Borghese.

"A fitting way to end it," he said.

"I know a more fitting way," she said and threw her arms around him.

"Larkey, this is a marble floor—"

"With you it will be ermine."

And, before the still, white eyes of Pauline Borghese, they made love. Their sighs must have echoed, because Norman heard from another room, "Who is there? Is anybody there?"

Larkey whispered into his ear. "A guard! Just be still and he will never see us."

Dressed again, they tiptoed to the main entrance. The lone guard stood at the door, his back to them.

Larkey shouted, "Oh, Norman, *there* is the door!"

The guard wheeled around. "What the hell are you doing here?" he asked.

"We have been lost," Larkey told him. "We have been lost

for the longest time, walking around in this maze of rooms. It is disgraceful that you do not have somebody here who can lead visitors to the door!"

Subdued and shaking his head, the guard let them out, and they laughed all the way back to the car.

"Our next stop is the Forum."

"What surprises do you have planned for us there?" he asked. "Are we going to defile the Temple of the Vestal Virgins?"

She laughed. "You must think I'm dreadful."

He nodded several times and they both laughed.

She took him first to the top of the Palatine Hill, and in the approaching darkness he picked poppies for her. Through the maze of old houses and down ancient staircases they walked until they reached the Forum itself. Not another soul was there, and Norman felt now that he and Larkey had gone back to the beginning of Rome.

"There, right over there," she said, pointing at three small marble columns joined at the top by a carved section of marble, "there is your precious Temple of the Vestal Virgins."

"This?" he said. "This tiny thing?"

"That's all that's left."

"You couldn't fit more than three virgins up there, and they'd have to be pretty small."

"Do you know three virgins these days, Norman?" She laughed. "The Gould sisters? Or do you think?" She laughed again. "Well, I am certainly no longer eligible."

He smiled. "That's why I love you."

They picked more flowers, sat on two-thousand-year-old broken columns and kissed.

"Come," she said, pointing at the magnificently preserved temple ahead of them whose marble columns looked like gnarled gray wood. He looked up to its soaring top, across which was carved "DIVO-ANTONINO-ET-DIVA-E-FAUSTINA EX-S.C." She led him up the long brick staircase, at the top of which they examined the stone bust of a man. Nearby was the bottom half of another. They leaned against it and kissed as wild flowers growing through the stones around them swayed in the gentle wind.

Larkey motioned behind them. Set into the wall of the temple and a third of the way up was a small metal balcony. "We have a visitor," she said. "I won't be able to attack you now."

Norman looked up at the tiny figure on the balcony. "I'm sorry to hear that," he said.

Now she threw her arms around him. "I don't really care what she thinks."

"Neither do—" He stared at the little balcony again, his eyes suddenly feeling like telescopes. The lady standing there was Pearlie Gish. She smiled at him and waved, then her eyes grew serious and she began to shake her head. Inside his own head he heard a strange sound, a click, a warning, and he looked up to the top of the temple, then pushed Larkey away from him, down onto the ground, and fell on top of her, just as an enormous rock crashed inches away, pebbles raining all around them.

"What happened?" she asked.

"Something fell from the top, a rock," he said. "I pushed you because I felt it coming." Once more he looked toward the balcony. Pearlie was gone.

"But, Norman, it could have fallen on you!"

"We were lucky." He sighed. "Does this kind of thing happen often around here?"

"I do not think this has ever happened."

He inspected bits of the smashed object. "This isn't rock. It's a granite block. This temple wasn't made out of granite. What the—"

"It is possible they are doing some repair work up there," she said. "After all, Norman, it is quite old, you know."

"Let's leave," he said.

"Our nice white costumes are a little shabby at the moment," she said as they got back into the car. "But it will not matter where we are going."

"Where?"

"To my favorite place in the city."

After several minutes of driving they parked again, and she led him through a curving little street onto a magnificent piazza that looked four times the size of a football field.

Three fountains splashed musically and many people strolled around them.

"The Piazza Navona," she said. "And now we shall have dinner. I am hungry, even if you are not."

"I'm starved. Hey, Larkey, I don't have any money."

"You need not worry, my love. I was brought up in one of these buildings. Up there, see? And I am known to everybody here."

And I wonder how many of them are friends of Monk's too? he wondered.

They were seated at an outdoor table in one of the restaurants directly in front of the Piazza's central fountain. Norman stared at the heroic Bernini figures, one in each corner, at the carved animals in the fountain's interior, water spurting like liquid crystal from openings all around, and the mist clouded his eyes. I've never seen anything more beautiful in my life, he thought.

Larkey was greeted lavishly by the restaurant's employees, all of whom looked quizzically at Norman.

"This is Norman Dickens," she said. "He is a friend from the United States and has never before been to Rome, so I am his guide."

Then they made a fuss over him, the restaurant's owner taking him inside and pointing to the wall just behind the cash register. Between two large hand-painted bowls was a tiny framed portrait of the owner, about an inch all around.

"This is the work of Signorina Larkey when she was twelve years old." He kissed Larkey. "When she grew up, Larkey was everybody's daughter in the Piazza. And now, I shall serve you such a meal that you will never forget you were in Rome."

It was a glorious meal, washed down with more wine than Norman thought himself capable of drinking.

"I've never tasted any of these dishes at home," Norman said to the beaming owner. "I didn't know pasta had so many shapes."

"Pasta has as many shapes as love," the man said, backing away.

Norman smiled and took Larkey's hand. "Your friend is a poet," he said, then stared into her eyes. "Larkey, would you believe you've taught me that love is possible? You've made me able to feel, see, what I never thought existed, at least not for me." He looked again at the incredible fountain.

Steaming espresso was brought to the table and dishes of zabaglione put in front of them.

"Well," he said, "this is the first part of the meal I recognize." And then he dropped his spoon. Walking past the fountain, gaily dressed, each with a girl on his arm, were Ronnie and Freddie, his aunts' neighbors. Would he ever know how they got here? Or did he already know and not want to face it. They both looked at him and nodded very slightly, and he got the oddest feeling, that same kind of clicking he had heard in his head before the block of granite smashed down on the steps of the Temple of Antonino and Faustina, and, without really willing it, he knocked his plate of dessert to the ground. The splashing of the fountain absorbed the sound and even Larkey, looking into his eyes, didn't notice it was gone.

Surreptitiously he watched the yellow liquid flow across the stones of the Piazza, and then he saw a cat approach and smell it. The cat looked just like Albert, Elizabeth and Amy's tortoiseshell. He wanted to chase the animal away, but he didn't want Larkey to know.

"You are far away, Norman," he heard her saying through his haze of fear.

"I'm sorry, Larkey. Look at the way the water dances out of the fountain."

Larkey looked over, and he watched as the cat began licking the zabaglione from the ground.

"Rome is a city of fountains," she said, and he barely heard her. "I have seen all of them in my short lifetime, but this is my favorite. Sometimes I cry when I leave it. Isn't it nice that we are sitting here?"

The cat stopped licking, threw itself onto the ground and began feebly tearing at its mouth with its front paws. Almost as quickly, it stopped moving and fell over on its back and its eyes closed. Norman gasped.

"What is it, Norman?"

He could feel freezing droplets of perspiration running down his chest. "Larkey, I want to leave now. I want to get back to the house. Right now."

Norman almost pulled her from the Piazza and drove crazily out of the city. The Colosseum and all the other awesome sights of Rome lost their magnificence, becoming only obstacles to get by on their way. God knows how many spies Monk has and where they are, he thought, but he's trying to kill me. I can't tell her. I won't ruin what we have left.

"Norman, you are driving so fast I fear for our safety."

He didn't slow down until they pulled off Appia Antica onto the Ferromonte estate.

Renzo and the Gould sisters were sitting on the ground on the near side of the pond, and their laughter seemed to carry him and Larkey across the lawn. Even from a distance he could see the black swan in the center of the pond, still, as though frozen, peering at him.

The girls exclaimed at seeing them and Renzo said, "We had given you up for lost. Have you had a good day?"

"Extraordinary," said Norman.

"It was the best day of our lives," said Larkey.

"Your wedding day is your best day, I've been told," said Amy, and Larkey gripped Norman's arm.

"What about people who get married several times?" drawled Maria.

"Forgive my baby sister," said Elizabeth. "Really Maria, you give absurdity a new meaning."

Renzo said, "I've been trying to convince the ladies that we should try to stay awake all night on this spot. I have placed a wager that I can outlast them, but they will not play."

"You don't have to look beautiful in the morning," said Elizabeth. Oh, Aunt Elizabeth, Norman thought, what have you become? "Well, enough of this gaiety," she added. "I say we are all to go to bed right now. Amy, help me up."

Amy stood up and helped Elizabeth.

"Why couldn't you get up by yourself?" asked Maria. "Are you putting us into training as servants to the new Signora Ferromonte?"

"When I decide what I'm going to do with you I'll inform you," said Elizabeth. She laughed again, and they all headed for the house.

Signe sat in the center of the pond and stared at Norman as they passed. He nodded and she swam to the far corner.

At the foot of the main staircase the Gould girls said good-night and Elizabeth impulsively threw her arms around Renzo and kissed him.

"I hope you'll all forgive my scandalous behavior," said Elizabeth, looking at Larkey and Norman. "But I feel I must join in the fun of at least some of the people in this house."

"Imagine what she'd do to me if I had said that," Maria drawled. Larkey looked at Norman, and he motioned for her to join the girls.

"Renzo," he said, "would it be all right if we had a drink in the drawing room?"

Over a glass of wine Norman told Renzo about the day's events.

Renzo nodded solemnly. "There was no coincidence and there is no repair work being done in the Forum. It is typical of the activities of Monk's associates. I fear for your life, Norman. Perhaps you should leave the country tonight." You don't know how easily that's done, Renzo, Norman thought.

"Not without saying goodbye to Larkey. And when I do, I might as well be dead anyway."

"Norman, I envy you more for these few days of love than

for anything else in my life I could have wished for. I am too upset to continue talking. Let us retire. I shall think of something by tomorrow." He stared at Norman. "Perhaps you should not leave this house tomorrow."

"I'll do whatever Larkey wants. I don't want to alarm her. Renzo, Larkey has told me this marriage is irreversible. I don't believe it, but if she goes through with it, let her just resent him, not hate him for trying to kill me."

"I shall never forgive myself if harm comes to you, Norman."

"But I'll forgive you, Renzo. And that's more important." He put his arm on Renzo's shoulder and they went up the stairs together.

Norman walked into his room, intending to bathe before going in to Larkey.

"Psst!" he heard in the darkness.

"Who is it?" he demanded.

"Who were you expecting?" came Larkey's voice from the bed.

He walked over and she threw her arms around him. "I have waited a long time for you. What were you and Renzo discussing?"

"His wedding."

She was quiet for a while. "I do not think that is a marriage made in heaven," she said. "But, then, I am the last person to make such comment."

He touched her bare skin and they stopped talking.

"You were much less gentle this time," she said. "It is a new kind of excitement, even if a little wearing."

"I'm sorry, Larkey. I was angry."

"With me?"

"No, with the unfairness of life."

"Norman, I know that you and I shall meet in an afterlife."

He laughed. Even if he told her the truth, she would never believe him. "Why don't you think Renzo and Elizabeth's marriage is made in heaven?"

"Because the stories about Lorenzo Ferromonte and his

148

special interests have been known around Rome for some time. Monk jokes about it constantly. I think, in all my wisdom of nineteen years, that perhaps an understanding and kind woman could deal with this, could even sway him."

"And you don't think Elizabeth is kind and understanding?

"I think Elizabeth is smart, even brilliant. And beautiful. But she is not kind. Amy would be a better wife for Renzo."

"Amy might not be smart enough to cope with him."

"She is loving enough. Well, we are beginning to sound like two fishwives in Trastevere."

"I love you, my fishwife," he whispered, kissing her gently on the ear.

That was the last he remembered before the incredible sounds in his head woke him up. The meowing of cats, just as on the first day he had landed in the Ferromonte garden. He dressed quickly, carried the sleeping Larkey to her room wrapped in a blanket, deposited her gently on her bed and raced across the lawn.

Even through the horrendous yowling, he heard Signe's call as he passed the pond, and he nodded at her as he rushed for the bushes.

16

He pushed his way through and heard Natalie's voice in the dining room.

"You obsolete creatures think you're going to keep me away from there forever, don't you?"

"Please, Natalie," he heard Aunt Elizabeth say. "You just don't understand. It hasn't been the proper time."

"Proper time, Signora Ferromonte? What do you really know about proper time?"

Norman slammed the door open and all three women started.

"What are *you* doing here?" he demanded of Natalie, who was wearing a black lace veil around her hair.

"Why, Norman"—she smiled—"where've you been? At Grandpa's house? Did you have a good time there?"

"We aren't going there any more," Amy blurted out, then covered her mouth.

"Oh?" Natalie raised an eyebrow and smiled at Norman. "Have you taken the ladies on a holiday?"

He stared at her and barely controlled herself from hitting her. "I asked you what you're doing in my aunts' house! Are you going to tell me or shall I call the police?"

Natalie laughed her "Hmm, hmm, hmm" laugh, and Amy buried her head in Elizabeth's chest. "You don't want police up here, Norman," Natalie said malevolently. "I don't think they would really understand some of the goings-on, do you?"

"Get out of this house," he said.

"But, Norman, all I wanted to do was just visit Simon Gould's house one more time."

"I said get out of this house." He stared at her with such hate that she gasped, then she began to cry. "Oh, Norman, forgive me for being so rude and nasty to your lovely aunts. It's just that— Please let me go there one more time. It was so beautiful." Now she covered her face, sobbing into her hands. "Why do you deny an old lady a little joy? Do you know what my life has been like, day after day in that grocery store? The only good day I had was that time Elizabeth and Amy let me go into the back room." She began to wipe her tears away, and he thought, All she is is an old lady after all.

"I'm sorry, Natalie, not now," he said gently.

"Please, Norman, I'll do anything. I'll give you anything,

Norman. I'm the one who gave them Signe, and it was Signe who brought them all the luck." Now her mysterious smile was back. "Have you seen Signe lately, Norman?"

He stared at her.

"I know a good deal more than you give me credit for," she whispered very quickly.

"Natalie, please leave," he said wearily. "We're all very tired now, and maybe tomorrow or the next day we can talk about it. O.K.?"

Her eyes seized on his. "You don't intend to talk about it to me ever, do you? I know your kind. Well, Mr. Norman Dickens, you can keep your precious back room. I won't demean myself any further by asking favors of you. But just remember this moment, Norman." She broke into her strange laugh and stormed out.

Both old ladies threw themselves on Norman.

"Oh, Norman, darling," Amy said, "she's going to come back. She's so evil, she's capable of anything."

He was deadly calm. "But still not capable of getting into that room, obviously. Aunt Amy, have I let anything happen to you so far?"

Elizabeth sighed loudly. "He's right, Amy. We have to believe in Norman now. What choice have we? Norman, how did you know she was here?"

"I didn't. I just heard the loud yowling in my head, the same yowling I heard on that first day." Now he remembered something and rushed into the kitchen. Three cats sat huddled together on one of the tables. Albert was nowhere in sight. "Aunt Amy!" he shouted, and Amy came through the lace curtain. "Where is Albert?"

"Albert? I don't know," she said feebly. "Probably hiding somewhere. Why, Norman?"

"No reason." Albert will never come out again, Aunt Amy.

Elizabeth began to moan. "Oh, Norman, oh, Norman." She fell down onto the bed, clutching her heart.

"What's the matter, Aunt Elizabeth?"

"I don't know. It hurts so."

"Can I get you something?"

"Just a little water."

As she gulped the water he asked, "How did Natalie get in here?"

"Amy and I were asleep in our rooms in the Ferromonte house when we heard the same loud yowling and we rushed back here and found her in the kitchen. She said she had knocked on the door and when we didn't answer she tried it and it was open so she came in. I hope you can keep that devil away from the back room. Oh, Norman, our house was so beautiful, no wonder she wants to go back. Can you remember it? It was even more beautiful than the Ferromonte house."

Norman's head felt as though it were turning at a thousand miles an hour, about to break off. He could never remember such pain and such a feeling of sorrow.

". . . And the garden. Oh, Norman, when you were little—"

And without warning, Norman was looking at Norman. He stared at the incredibly beautiful child with the black hair and blue eyes in the spectacular garden of Grandpa Simon's castle. Everybody was looking at the little boy, who now began to cry. He blinked and there was only one Norman now.

"Mama," he heard himself saying, "I don't like Grandpa's house today." He couldn't stop his crying.

"Norman, baby," said Auntie Elizabeth, rushing up to him, her skirt making that nice sound and her perfume surrounding him. "You're always so happy here, darling. What can be the matter?"

"I'm not happy today," he heard himself saying, and he continued to cry. He couldn't, didn't know how to tell them that the moving pictures in his head showed him that his grandfather had just died upstairs. He stood still and cried. "Mama, please take me home."

"In a little while, darling," Mama told him.

But Norman didn't want to wait and he ran from them and hid in the hydrangea bushes. He stayed there until he heard a scream upstairs and crying from all over the house. Finally he walked out into the empty garden. And he vowed he would never cry again.

Now Norman stood in the doorway of the back room sobbing his heart out. Elizabeth and Amy threw their arms around him.

"How did I get there?" he asked.

"I don't know," said Elizabeth, crying with him. "All I know is that I was wishing you would see our old house again. I wanted to reward you for saving us from Natalie."

"And the reward was to bring me back to one of the most unhappy days of my life?"

"Norman, darling, we had no control." She gripped his arm. "I notice you got us out of there fast enough. The control is all in your hands now."

"Oh, Norman, what are we going to do now?" Amy asked.

"Do? What do we *have* to do?"

Elizabeth sank to the bed again. "Norman, I hope you can do something soon. I don't think I'm going to last. I'm not play-acting. I have such pains in my chest."

He walked over to the bed. "Let me help you up, Aunt Elizabeth."

"Why?"

"Because we're going to Renzo's house."

"How do we know we can get back so soon?"

"Don't worry, we will," he said and pushed on the door, which swung open.

The frightened eyes relaxed and Aunt Elizabeth smiled.

"Oh, good," said Amy as he led the two of them through the branches.

17

It was barely light in the garden. "Oh, Norman!" called Elizabeth as she and Amy drifted toward him wearing matching negligees. "Amy, look, another insomniac."

They came up to him, these two beautiful women. "We both woke up and couldn't fall asleep again. I think it was the noise of the swans or something, so we decided to take a stroll. My, the dew is bone-chilling. Shall we walk back together?"

He escorted them to the house, noticing as he passed the pond that Signe was asleep, her long neck curled around her body, her head buried in her feathers.

He tiptoed into Larkey's room, and she opened her eyes as soon as he reached the bed.

"Norman, how did I get here?" She held her arms out to him.

"You know what, Norman? Let us bathe and dress now and go out early. We'll breakfast in the city and spend the whole day there, our last day. Now go back to your room and call for me shortly."

He kissed her and returned to his room, where he bathed and then looked at yesterday's clothes in disgust. He was about to put them on, when he moved to the closet and opened it. It was filled with clothing. Renzo's? What difference did it make?

He put on a navy suede suit, with a white silk shirt and navy tie.

As he was about to walk out the door, he found an envelope on the floor, addressed to him.

Signor Dickens:

Signor Ferromonte has instructed me to be your driver and guide for the day. I will be at the garage, awaiting your pleasure.

Paolo

So Renzo had thought of something. A driver who would also be a bodyguard. Good old Renzo. In some faraway place in his mind he thought of Natalie breaking into the apartment again, but in this world it didn't really matter.

Larkey was wearing a silky rose-colored dress, with the diamond stickpin at her bosom. On the way across the lawn to the garage he picked a pink rose, which he linked through the catch of the pin.

A tall muscular man in a smart gray uniform leaned against a sparkling black Rolls-Royce and saluted as they approached.

"Good morning, Signori, I am Paolo." He smiled. Norman relaxed for the first time since last evening on the Piazza Navona. Paolo looked as though he could cope with anything Monk Abruzzi's aides might have in mind.

At Larkey's bidding he drove them into Trastevere.

"It means 'across the Tiber,'" she said, "and it is where you will really see Rome."

Over Paolo's objections, she insisted he park and wait in the car while they wandered the curving narrow streets, crowded with shabby ochre and brown buildings, and watched Rome slowly wake up.

"Today I brought money." She smiled. From outdoor stands they bought their breakfast—cheese, bread, sausage and wine—and ate as they walked.

"It has not really been my habit to drink wine for breakfast," Larkey said.

"Oh, I do it all the time," he said.

"You are perhaps related to our little Maria Gould?" He laughed along with her, thinking, Larkey, if you only knew how funny that is.

"Well," she said, "I can buy us another bottle."

"You've bought me enough. Back home they would call me a kept man."

"But here I cannot keep you," she answered sadly.

They strolled for more than an hour, Norman occasionally looking above them to see whether anything was poised to fall.

When they came to the end of Trastevere, they walked out to the river, and waiting for them was Paolo in the car. Paolo, he thought, our good luck charm.

Larkey next told the driver to take them to the Church of Santa Maria Maggiore.

"Rome has many famous churches," she said as they mounted the steps, "but this has always been my special one."

Norman shivered at the beautiful other-worldly sound of the choir as they entered. They walked quietly along the side aisle, passing swiftly moving white-coated fathers, until they stopped at a statue under which was engraved, "Ave Regina Paces." The Virgin held the Child with one hand; the other was thrust out.

"Is she beckoning or warning us away?" Norman asked.

Larkey shrugged. "Which do you want?"

Now they moved to the center portion of the cathedral, whose floors were of marble in multiple designs. The dome above the altar was made entirely of mosaics featuring the Redeemer, the Mother and a group of angels. While he studied it, he felt Larkey's grasp tighten on his hand and he realized a wedding was in progress. They stared dumbfounded as the priest sing-songed in Latin and blessed the kneeling couple.

This is the last thing I needed, thought Norman. Larkey leaned her head against him and wiped her tears on his sleeve. When the ceremony ended, the glorious choir began singing again. Larkey pointed to the ceiling and Norman gasped. The entire vast area was filled with squares, in the center of each of which stood what looked like a giant gold flower.

"They are made with the gold said to have been brought by Columbus from the New World, from your world," said Larkey.

If only I could bring you into my world, he thought.

"Now," she said, taking his hand and looking wistfully at the bride and groom as they kissed the guests in the receiving line, "I shall show you a sight so dazzling that even you will be amazed."

She gave Paolo instructions and they settled into the back seat. "Where are we going?"

"You shall see," she said and kissed him.

They drove for nearly an hour, through mountains and little villages, until they came upon the prettiest village of all. She told Paolo to stop the car.

"Now you shall see the Tivoli fountains," she said, and they wandered through the village until they came to a castle. She led him quickly through the rooms until they walked out to the gardens.

Norman blinked. She had been right. It was dazzling.

"There are hundreds of fountains here," she said as he stared in wonder. "The water goes every way possible—and even some ways not possible."

Hand in hand, they walked through the sculpted greenery, stopping to admire the ingeniously designed bursts of water all around them. They came to one man-created waterfall with fountains coursing from all sides.

"Under there is where I would like to make love," said Larkey.

"Marble is one thing, drowning is another," said Norman, and they laughed. Some of the other visitors stared at them.

When several hours had gone by and they were tired, they sat on a bench under a tree, not speaking, resting against each other.

Our last day, he thought. Thank you, Renzo, for sending somebody along to watch over us.

Just as he was about to get up, Larkey stopped him and removed two small pens from her purse. "Close your eyes," she said.

For several moments he felt pressure against his thumbnail. "What are you doing?" he asked.

"You shall see. Now, open your eyes."

He looked down at his left thumbnail, which now contained, in intricately worked ink, a picture of a peony.

"A souvenir of me," she said.

On the way back to the car he was jolted by a thought: Fulcho. He hadn't gone home last night to feed Fulcho. Well, he'd left him an enormous plateful of cat food. He would survive. Living in two worlds was not the easiest thing after all. He wondered whether Elizabeth and Amy were at the Ferromonte house or back in their furniture jungle.

"Now for lunch," Larkey said and gave Paolo new directions. They drove a short distance until they stopped at a small inn, where they were led to a garden which looked out upon mountains and valleys and was bounded on both sides by ancient walls whose bricks looked like honeycombs.

"Those walls are more than two thousand years old," she said. He stared ahead at the unbelievable beauty of the valleys, with their little houses and gardens, their grapevines and olive trees.

The smiling waiter brought them a parade of delicacies, and they ate and drank in silence.

"Now is a good time for a nap," she said. Norman walked over to the proprietor, who assured them that, yes, he had some rooms above the restaurant and that—with the slyest of winks —he understood how the signor and his wife would need to rest and relax after a long day of sightseeing.

The tiny room with the sagging bed had only two advantages —its door had a bolt lock and it overlooked the mountains. Looking out, Norman realized the inn had been built right into the ancient wall, and from their window it was a sheer drop to the valley.

The proprietor could have saved all his winking. Exhausted from their walk and drowsy with wine, they were asleep within seconds.

Norman's dreams were a kaleidoscope of this world and his own, with characters intermingled, changing parts, as in a surrealistic movie. In extreme closeup he saw Dr. Morgan smoking his pipe placidly, to be replaced by Natalie and her mocking face, who then became Linda reading her farewell note aloud. And then Linda became Sharon. Next he saw Elizabeth and Amy and Maria walking hand in hand, and suddenly they became the Elizabeth and Amy of 1973—and Maria's face was the one he had seen in her coffin. End this dream, Norman, he heard himself say, end this dream. But it wasn't his own voice he heard any more, it was the voice of Dr. Fredric Morgan. End this dream, Norman, wake up.

His eyes snapped open and he looked quickly around the room. The door's bolt was still in place. No danger. Again he heard that clicking in his head and he looked toward the window and noticed the top of a rope ladder poking into the room. He crawled across the bed to the window, leaned against the wall and peered out. Moving swiftly up the ladder, just a few feet below, was a man. In a few seconds, measured out like years by Norman's pounding pulse, the face of the man was level with the window, one hand hanging on to the ladder, the other holding a gun. Norman remained concealed. The man raised himself so he was looking right into the window and aimed the gun at the sleeping figure under the blanket. Instantly Norman moved away from the wall and gave the man a violent blow across his eyes. The intruder gasped almost soundlessly and fell back and Norman heard the echoing screams as he fell thousands of feet into the valley. He freed the end of the rope ladder, allowing it to join its owner.

First he talked himself under control, then he tapped Larkey. "Wake up, little one. It's almost dark and we have to go back."

"Oh, Norman, what a sweet rest," she said, holding out her arms.

"Larkey, it's very late."

"It's also the last time," she said.

In the remaining light he stared at her body, trying to memorize it. He smiled grimly to himself. I've traveled backward and forward between two worlds, he thought, and I can't think of a way to stay with this girl.

On the way back to the car Larkey whispered, "Paolo will

159

probably be in a state of shock for months. Respectable Roman ladies do not behave this way." And Norman thought Paolo would be even more shocked if he knew how close his charges had come to death at the hands of one more of Monk Abruzzi's associates.

The chauffeur was sitting in the car and seemed astonished at seeing them.

"Look at his face." Larkey laughed. And when they got to the car, Norman said, "I'm sorry we were away so long, but we got tired and fell asleep."

"Signor," said Paolo, "can you tell me where you plan to go next?"

Norman looked at Larkey.

"I think we will go back to the Ferromonte house," she said, "and on the way, Norman, I shall take you for a short visit to the Baths of Caracalla."

Paolo excused himself, saying he had promised to call Signor Ferromonte to let him know when his passengers could be expected.

It was dark by the time they got back into the city and Paolo edged the car silently up to the entrance to the Baths of Caracalla. Norman checked the rearview mirror to make sure no cars were behind them.

As they approached the entrance, Norman marveled at the lush trees, some giant, others tiny.

"They are like families of trees," Larkey said. "In your country do you have a child's story called 'The Three Bears'? I always think of these as the Bear trees."

Inside the Baths, by moonlight, Larkey pointed out the ancient walls and he picked poppies for her and they kissed for a long time.

"Do I still remind you of your cat with the fiery name?" she asked.

"Yes. You even have the same color eyes. But he's prettier."

She laughed. "We'd better go. It would be just like Monk to telephone tonight from Palermo." *To find out if I've been killed yet, Larkey.*

They had barely driven away from the entrance to the Baths when the car stopped. Paolo jerked the choke in and out, then slapped his hand on the dashboard. "I am the fool of the world," he said to Norman. "We have run out of petrol and I must now search for someplace to get some."

He opened the door for them. "In case you want to stroll until I return with the petrol." He saluted and walked back in the direction of the city.

"Shall we go back into the Baths?" Larkey asked.

"Yes," he said and kissed her.

Her eyes shone at him and suddenly they seemed like Fulcho's eyes, yesterday, when Norman had shouted while Aunt Amy held the telephone the wrong way. Again he got that clicking feeling inside his head and he wheeled around just as Larkey screamed and they were knocked to the ground. At first it seemed like a hundred men attacking them. Larkey's screams became muffled and he knew somebody had his hands over her mouth. Another one was sitting on Norman's stomach, his hand over his mouth, while a third was about to come down on Norman's face with his boot. Norman bit hard and the one on his stomach let out an animal shriek, giving Norman just enough time to push him off and jump up again. With all his force, while the injured one was moaning, he leaped at the third, battering his head into the man's chest. Like a deflating punching bag, the man fell to the ground and Norman heard his head hit the pavement. Something glinted in the man's hand, and Norman removed the knife he'd been holding and now went for the one dragging Larkey along the ground toward the entrance to the Baths.

"Let her go!" Norman said. "Let her go or I'll kill you!" He rushed at the man, who dropped Larkey and whipped out a gun, which he was just about to aim when Norman leaped on him and jabbed the knife so far into the man's chest that his hand throbbed with pain. The shriek from the dying man was the second scream he knew he'd hear in his head for the rest of his life.

Larkey fell against him. "Are you all right, Norman? Have they hurt you?"

"I'm O.K., Larkey. There's a third one, the one whose hand I bit. We'd better see what happened to—"

They heard the sound of the car's engine as it drove away. On the ground were the bodies of the men he'd knocked down. The third was gone.

"He must have gotten the car started somehow. How could he?"

"Shall we wait here for Paolo?" Larkey asked.

"No," he said, "let's get back to the house. Let's walk."

Arm in arm, they staggered along the road until it narrowed into Via Appia Antica.

"If they intended robbery, they were disappointed," Larkey said.

"I don't think robbery was what they had in mind."

"What, then?"

"I'm not sure. It doesn't matter. We're safe, that's all I care about."

Through the moonlight they passed the silent tombs and statues on Appia Antica and finally walked into the Ferromonte garden.

In the darkness they heard "Larkey, is that you?"

Renzo appeared. "I've been worried almost to my grave about the two of you," he said. "From early morning, when you disappeared."

"Disappeared?" Larkey asked. "Didn't you know when the car was gone that we had left for the city?"

Renzo stared at Larkey, then at Norman.

"None of my cars was gone," he said softly.

Norman's eyes widened. "But your chauffeur, Paolo, told us— You don't have a chauffeur named Paolo, do you?"

Renzo shook his head and Larkey gasped.

"I have been the fool of the world," she said, "the blind fool of the world, to think that Monk Abruzzi would let my last days go unnoticed."

"But you're back, thank Jesus," said Renzo, then stared at their clothing.

"Three men leaped on us right near the Baths of Caracalla," Norman said. "Three men in the employ of Monk Abruzzi, who were tipped off by his other valuable employee, Paolo, the chauffeur who isn't a chauffeur."

"What happened to them?" Renzo asked.

"I stabbed one of them," Norman said. "He's dead. I heard the second one's head crack as he hit the ground. The third one disappeared." He saw no sense in mentioning the fourth, whose body was at the bottom of the valley.

Renzo covered his eyes with his hands. "That explains it." He shivered.

"Explains what?" Norman asked.

"Monk is in the house," Renzo answered. Larkey gasped. "He has been here for several hours, first demanding to know where Larkey was. I told him I had no idea, that she'd probably gone into the city with the Gould sisters. I haven't seen them since this morning either, but that is their way. Then about an hour ago he received a telephone call which sent him into a violent rage. He was shouting something about the stupidity of the person on the other end. I heard him say, 'Killing cats is the most you're good for,' before he hung up. He is storming around the house. I ran out here to get away from him. Also to see whether you might, by some miracle, show up."

"Killing cats?" Larkey asked. She stared at Norman, who said nothing.

"She might as well know it all, Norman," Renzo said, and he told Larkey the truth about the granite block in the Forum and the poisoned dessert on the Piazza Navona.

Larkey's eyes narrowed and Norman felt her body tense against him.

"So, he is in the house," she hissed. "He who expects to be my husband tomorrow and has attempted to murder me tonight. His anger is as nothing compared to that of the Princess Fabbro." She lifted her head and swept quickly across the lawn.

"Princess?" Renzo asked.

Norman nodded.

163

They followed Larkey as she stormed up the marble steps of the house and slammed the front door open.

"Monk!" she screamed. "Monk, are you here?"

"Is she mad?" Renzo asked.

A clatter came from the ballroom and Monk walked through the doorway.

Larkey strode over to him, followed by Norman and Renzo.

"So there you are!" Monk shouted angrily.

"So there *you* are!" Larkey shouted back.

He stared at Norman. "You were told to stay away from Larkey."

"It is Larkey who chose to stay with him," she said. "And it is the same Larkey who demands to know why you have loosed your thugs to try to kill us."

Monk raised his eyebrows.

"Yes, kill us," she said. "Your three gangsters who leaped upon us when your chauffeur disappeared. Is this one of the tender acts of love you promised, my bridegroom? Is it?"

"I didn't—" He stared at Norman now and said, "If my Renaldo were not such a slow climber you would not be here at all."

"Who?" Larkey asked.

"Your Renaldo will never climb again," Norman said. "He's sleeping at the bottom of the valley."

Monk's eyes bulged.

"What is this?" Larkey asked Norman.

"One of Signor Abruzzi's associates was a mountain climber who tried to reach us at the inn before. I reached him first."

Larkey turned to Monk again. "You listen to me, Signor Abruzzi. As of this moment our engagement is ended. I do not fear you or your thugs and I no longer wish to associate with you. I cannot be concerned about the financial welfare of my parents when I know the money comes from a murderer. Now, I want you to leave this house."

"You have no choice in the matter," Monk said, grabbing Larkey and pulling her into the ballroom. "Now, if you will have the good sense to listen to me, I will tell you why."

Larkey tried to pull away. "I have no intention of listening to anything else you have to say!"

Monk let her arm fall and smacked her across the face.

Norman leaped into the ballroom and, with one violent movement, knocked Monk to the floor, then pushed Larkey out of the way. Monk was on his feet almost immediately and his fist connected with Norman's left eye. Norman backed away and was about to rush him again when Monk toppled a statue over at him. Trying to avoid it, Norman slid to the ground, and thousands of marble slivers bounced around him. Monk was standing over him with a chair raised above his head when Larkey screamed.

The distraction gave Norman enough time to jab a sharp splinter of the smashed statue into Monk's ankle. He let out a cry as Norman jumped up. Then Monk pulled a gun from his pocket.

What next possessed Norman he would never know. Whether it was the remembered skill of military training—or the one crazy not-caring act of his life. He kicked his right leg up, connected with Monk's hand, and deflected the gun as it was going off. The bullet whipped into the far wall, and Norman, like a maniac, grabbed Monk and hit him in the face again and again, then shoved him violently forward. There was an immense crash and he realized he had pushed Monk through the priceless stained-glass wall.

Larkey and Renzo ran over to him.

"Renzo, I've ruined your wall," Norman said.

"Who cares? The Ferromonte family will buy another."

"The Ferromonte family will not live to buy anything," said Monk. He crawled across the glass-strewn floor and came up to them, blood all over his face and hands. Larkey gasped. "Well, my bride," he said. "And you will be my bride tomorrow, you see. Jesus only knows why I should still want you, but that is the peculiarity which makes me what I am. You see, Larkey, as bold as I am"—he wiped his hands across his face, smearing the blood—"I never do anything without insurance. Your parents are being held in a house somewhere in Rome. They will be freed tomorrow evening—in time to attend our wedding." With great effort, he stood up and leaned against one of the statues. A less majestic pose than the other night, Norman thought, but just as arrogant.

Larkey began to cry.

"I thought you would get the drift of my conversation," continued Monk. "You see, if there is no wedding, there will be no parents to attend it. They will vanish without a trace. You called me a murderer before, my bride. Murderer will not be a strong enough word when it comes to dealing with your parents." He laughed. "Now I shall leave." He looked at Renzo. "Tomorrow I will tell you how I intend to deal with your part in this little conspiracy." He lifted Larkey's chin. "Do not cry, my love. I expect you in my home tomorrow afternoon at three instead of seven. I want you there early. You see, I have decided to sample some of your favors in advance of our wedding." He looked at Norman and smiled. "You fight well, but you must lose when you fight against Monk Abruzzi. And if I were you I would keep a sharp eye on members of my family. You see, Norman, Renaldo—the mountain climber—was my brother, and as soon as my associates get the proper information about your family it shall be an eye for an eye."

He turned again to Larkey. "Do not think that when I leave I will not know what is going on here. I want this murdering gigolo out of the house in no more than ten minutes, or your beloved mother will attend our wedding minus a foot."

And he left the house.

Norman put his arms around Larkey and tried to soothe her. Renzo patted her hair.

"Oh, Norman," she cried, "I have dragged you into this mess along with me. And you too, Renzo."

"Don't worry, Larkey," Renzo said quietly. "The Ferromonte family still has some power in Italy—enough even to combat the forces of Signor Abruzzi."

"And what about you, Norman?" She sobbed. "What about your family?"

"My family will be safe," Norman said. "Larkey, if you want me to go after him—"

"No, no more!" she cried and fell against him, hysterical.

Norman and Renzo led her into the drawing room and Renzo made her drink some wine.

"I know what I must do," she said. "Exactly as Monk says. Renzo, please have a car ready for tomorrow at two thirty to take me to his house. Perhaps I can plead with him not to carry out his threats against the two of you." She put her hands on Norman's cheeks. "Norman, you must say goodbye to me."

"No," Norman said feebly.

She kissed him. "We have only time to say goodbye." She stood up. "I shall see you to the door."

Norman looked at Renzo, whose face was devoid of expression. Renzo's stare followed him as he walked out the door with Larkey.

At the entrance to the house Larkey put her arms around Norman and kissed him again. "Goodbye, my Norman. I thank you for the privilege of loving you." Tears were streaming down her face.

"Larkey, I'll come back."

She put her hand over his mouth. "You must go. You know you must." She kissed him again, for a long time, then turned and rushed across the hallway to the staircase. He watched her disappear, looked around the empty entrance hall, then left the house.

Through gritted teeth he tasted the salt of his tears as he walked slowly across the thick grass. He glanced over at Signe, whose call sounded like a wail.

He reached the bush at the edge of the garden and turned around to stare at the flowers awash in moonlight, the silent swans in the pond, the beautiful Ferromonte house. Was Larkey standing on her balcony? He couldn't make it out, and he walked through the bush and into 1973.

18

He squinted, even at the little amount of light in the dining room.

"Oh, Elizabeth," Amy was saying, "I'm so hungry."

Norman walked into the room.

"Norman, you startled me," Elizabeth said.

"Norman?" Amy called from the kitchen. "Is he back?"

"No, I just like to talk to imaginary people named Norman. Really, Amy! Norman, I'm so happy to see you."

Amy hobbled in and both of them stared at him. He touched his face, still wet with tears, then looked at his hand. Larkey's little thumb drawing was smeared away.

"Norman, why don't you say something?" Amy said.

"Hello," he said softly.

"Look, Elizabeth, he has a black eye! How did you get a black eye, Norman?"

Norman felt as if he were nailed to the floor. He couldn't move and he couldn't talk.

"Norman, what happened?" Aunt Elizabeth asked.

"A lot of things," he said. "How long have you been back here?"

"Oh, we came back early this afternoon—" Amy began.

"Let me do the talking, Amy," said Elizabeth. "This afternoon —it was just before lunch—when Renzo noticed you and Larkey missing. I remember saying to Amy something like 'Well, maybe now we'll get Renzo's undivided attention for a change,' and then we heard the cats screaming and had to return here. And all day we've tried to get back." Now she clutched her heart again. "Oh, Norman, I'm sure if you'd been there with us we could have stayed. Are we being punished for something? I was afraid this would happen. It's that one in the grocery store!"

"Aunt Elizabeth, relax. I'll take care of everything." How? he wondered.

She almost gasped the next: "That's a very large order. Norman, we haven't eaten since this morning. We tried calling Pearlie and she was out all day, and Ronnie and Freddie were gone too. We're so hungry. Can you get us something to eat?"

He looked at his watch. "It's nine thirty. Is anything open?"

"Certainly, love, there's a delicatessen open until eleven down the block." Her voice was stronger now. "Here"—she reached for her purse—"be a good boy and run down there for us. Get us a double order of herring in cream sauce—make sure that thief goes heavy on the onions. I learned that from Pearlie—and . . ." She smiled. "Amy, you know what we haven't had in years? F.H.!"

"Oh, Lizbeth, I'm too hungry to guess. I give up."

"Fresh ham!" She turned to Norman. "They have the most scrumptious fresh ham on the continent. Have him carve us two of his famous sandwiches, with some ravishing cole slaw on the side."

"I don't like fresh ham," Amy said.

Elizabeth's look was sorrowful. "Yes you do, child. It's *baked* ham you don't like." She turned back to Norman. "She really is Elizabeth's little lamb, God love her. Well now, we'd also like two pieces of baklava. Amy, do we need anything else?"

"There's no sense in buying any more," Amy said, patting one of the cats at her feet. "I'm sure we'll have a good breakfast in Daddy's house tomorrow—or Renzo's house."

This grim scene, Norman thought, shifting every second from reality to fantasy.

"Don't be too sure of that." Elizabeth sighed and put her hand on her heart.

"Norman," said Amy, "when you get out to the street, will you look around for Albert? He's been missing since last night. I think he might have run out when Natalie came in."

Norman nodded. *He's lying dead in the Piazza Navona, Aunt Amy.*

He left the apartment quickly, followed by Elizabeth's cries of "Wait! Let me give you money."

Trudging down the block, not really feeling part of this world, he looked up at the moon. Are you there, Larkey? he wondered. Where are you? Then he laughed. Norman Dickens, the conqueror, the hero, he thought, after spending the two most wonderful days of his life, among the ancient walls and fountains of Rome, was headed for the corner delicatessen to quell the hunger pangs of his two crazy aunts. His laughter got louder and louder, careening around the corners of his brain. It only subsided when he forced himself to face the fact that his aunts, who for eight years had been traveling backward in time with hardly the blink of an eye, were still two old ladies who got hungry.

He opened the door with his own key as Amy was saying, "It was Joan Blondell, *not* Ginger Rogers, Elizabeth! You check and see."

"Ah, our champion with the vittles!" Elizabeth laughed.

Amy was now in her royal purple robe, with a green chiffon turban, and Elizabeth wore an old white negligee.

He was about to move the dishes cluttering the table when, on an impulse, he swept everything onto the floor. The three cats leaped away to avoid the crashing dishes.

"Are you possessed, love?" Elizabeth asked.

"I'm sorry, Aunt Elizabeth. It seemed like the easiest way to clear the table—and what the hell does it matter anyway?"

Amy nodded her head very quickly several times, like a child. "Yes, what the hell does it matter anyway?"

Norman opened the packages of food and watched these two birdlike creatures begin eating from the paper containers. They really are like ravenous birds, he thought. Ravenous sparrows who were once . . . He opened several cans of cat food and fed the screeching animals, noticing that the calico no longer had a dropped stomach.

"What did Victoria do with her kittens?" he asked.

Elizabeth shrugged.

"I think she might have put them into the back room," Amy said.

"They may be in Italy now," he said quietly, and both women smiled.

"Oh, Norman," Amy said, "it's such a pleasure talking to you like this. Now that we know we can trust you and that you're going to take care of us. We're not just relatives any more. We're friends now." She picked up the remainder of her sandwich and tucked it into her mouth.

"Yes, Norman," said Elizabeth. "Now why don't you tell a couple of friends what happened to you all day?"

Not quite rooted in reality, he told them the whole story. When he finished, the two old ladies had stopped eating and were crying quietly.

"I've never been so touched in my entire life," Elizabeth said.

"Oh, Norman," Amy sobbed, "that's the most beautiful story I ever heard. We never would have known if you hadn't been there."

"But none of us knows what happened to Larkey," Norman said. "None of us will." He said the rest automatically, feeling as if he were listening to somebody else talking. "I'm going back for her."

"Oh, Norman, Norman," sobbed Amy.

Through her tears Elizabeth whispered, "Norman, do you know the story of *Lost Horizon?*"

He nodded.

"Even if you could take Larkey back here, she would be sixty-four years old."

"How do you know?" he asked.

Elizabeth shrugged. "Do as you wish, Norman. I thank God I won't live to see it happen."

"Aunt Elizabeth, what happened to Renzo?"

Her eyes looked glazed. "Renzo? I don't really know. Years later we heard he got married again, but then we never heard any more. Ah, what's the use? I was probably the least naïve young woman in the world at the time, but when I caught him, my gargantuan ego just couldn't manage it. What a fool I was. What difference would it have made now? There was never a more wonderful man than Renzo. And he loved me so much in his own way. If I'd shown some understanding, some compassion, I might still be Signora Ferromonte. And my whole life would be different now. And so would hers." She nodded toward Amy. "Norman, this poor old world just never measured up to my standards, I'm afraid, and I didn't have the wit to change them. Well, it doesn't mean a damn any more. Amy, get the hatbox!"

"What hatbox?" Norman asked.

"You'll see," said Elizabeth as Amy went into the dining room and Elizabeth stared after her. He heard her rummaging around, then a crash.

"Watch it," Elizabeth said wryly. "Don't want any more cracks in our good china, do we?"

Amy emerged with an enormous black hatbox, faded and stained, rubber bands wound tightly around it. She put it on one of the chairs.

"This hatbox," Elizabeth said very solemnly, "contains everything valuable we own, which isn't very much. No, Norman, I'm not going to open it. We can't take a chance keeping it around here any more, what with that robbery at Freddie and Ronnie's. And I feel even more uneasy about Natalie breaking in here last night. There are things that must not— Excuse me, I'm rambling. Norman, now that you have earned our trust I want you to take it home with you tonight for safekeeping, and then when you come here tomorrow bring it with you. Come here before three o'clock and I'll send you to the neighborhood bank where I want you to open a safe deposit box for us and put it in. All right?"

Norman nodded. "If there's cash, maybe you ought to open a savings—"

"No," she said firmly. "I know exactly what I want to do. If anything happens to Amy or myself, you'll see that the other one is taken care of, and, naturally, you'll be our sole heir." Norman almost laughed out loud. "Now take this home with you, and I want you to promise that you won't look inside, that you'll just keep it overnight and bring it back with you tomorrow. You will come here tomorrow, won't you?"

"I'll be here any time you need me, Aunt Elizabeth."

"You sounded just like Daddy when you said that. Didn't he, Amy? Such determination. Daddy was the most determined man in the world. You really are a Gould through and through, Norman. Oh . . . oh . . ." She gripped her chest and began to gasp.

"What is it, Aunt Elizabeth?" She let her head fall back. Her eyes rolled up under the sockets, and all he saw were slits of white. "What's the matter?"

She shook her head. "Oh, Norman, I think I can't last much longer. I don't want to die and go to hell. I want to go to Daddy's house or, if you like, to Renzo's house. Oh, God, don't let me die, please!" Her head fell forward.

"Aunt Elizabeth, can I get you something?"

"Get me a new life," she whispered. "That's what I want for Christmas."

Amy sat down next to her sister and stroked her hair. "Oh, you'll be all right, Elizabeth, you'll see," she said, straining to keep calm. "Just tell yourself you'll be all right." Her voice began to break. "Elizabeth, dear, I'll bet anything you can't sing all the verses of 'The Twelve Days of Christmas.'" Tears streamed down her face and she looked at Norman helplessly. "How about it, Elizabeth?"

Elizabeth remained silent, then, with her head still resting on the table, she began to whisper, "On the first day of Christmas my true love gave to me, a partridge in a pear tree." Her voice got stronger and Amy smiled. "On the second day of Christmas my true love gave to me, two turtledoves and a partridge— Oh, Amy, I know every one of them. Sing with me." She raised her head and put her arms around Amy.

And together they began to sing, "On the third day of Christmas, my true love gave to me, three French hens, two turtledoves and a partridge in a pear tree."

Norman listened to the lovely voices of the two old women as they held on to each other, and they looked like the young beautiful Gould sisters again. I love you so much, my aunts, he said to himself. He didn't want to break the spell by saying goodbye.

On his way to the corner he looked into Berkenblitt's Bargains. It was dark and quiet and the shade was pulled down over the door, the "Closed for Religious Observation" sign pinned to its center.

He held the hatbox on his lap in the cab, astonished at its heaviness, dying to look inside, vowing to keep his promise.

Fulcho's screams reached him as he walked out of the elevator, and when he opened the door the cat leaped out into the hall, growling hoarsely, and walked away from him.

"Fulcho, come back."

Fulcho gave him a dirty look that made the dark brown portions of his face seem even darker.

"Come on back, Fulcho, and I'll explain."

With infinite dignity and his nose in the air, the cat walked back into the apartment, sniffed at the hatbox, and with great reluctance allowed Norman to scoop him up.

"That performance doesn't fool me," Norman said, "because you can't control the purring."

Fulcho capitulated and Norman rubbed his nose against the cat's, then carried him into the kitchen and put him on the counter, where the cat stood at attention and stared at him.

"I wonder how you'd look as a swan?" Norman asked. He felt Fulcho's cold eyes on him and fed him a large portion of chicken livers. Then he picked up the telephone and called Sharon.

"I thought you were dead by now," she said.

Maybe I am, Sharon. "I was there all weekend. I never left." *Except for a couple of trips to Italy and the delicatessen on the corner.* He bit his lip.

"What did you do there? You must be exhausted."

"They'd have to invent a new word for what I am, Sharon." He laughed. "It's a very long story. I'll tell you about it tomorrow, O.K.?"

"Sure, dear, whatever you like. Whenever you like."

Norman swallowed. She sounded just like Larkey.

"See you in the morning, Norman— Norman?"

"Sorry, I was drifting. Would you please give me Fred's home number?"

"Sure. I envy him, knowing so much about you. Norman, if you'd like me to come over and spend the night . . ." Even more like Larkey now.

As gently as he could, he said no and hung up.

He dialed Fred's number, staring at the tiny flower on the back of the stickpin, then unfolded the story of the weekend.

"Do you still want tangible proof, Fred? I have a black eye and bruises all over my body, and"—he laughed—"what was left of my mind is pretty well shot."

"I'm glad you can make jokes about it, Norman. What do you plan to do now?"

"I don't know. I have to go back, even if Larkey doesn't see me. I have to know what's going to happen."

Fred was silent for a long time. "Norman, you know your crazy aunt is right. Never mind the chapter I'm writing—I could do a whole book on you alone—but don't make any attempt to bring her back. I can't see you on the arm of a sixty-four-year-old woman."

Norman laughed again. "May-December romances sometimes last, Fred. Don't worry, I'll behave. We Goulds just wouldn't know another way."

He clutched the stickpin as he tried to fall asleep, but the moment he turned off the light all the strange happenings of the past week seemed to join hands and dance around him. A cat who turned into a swan. An old crone who became Cinderella at a ball. A weird grocery lady with some unknown power who had seduced his grandfather twenty years after his death. The only place he had some normalcy, he thought ironically, was in his office, Mr. Perry notwithstanding. Then he began to wonder about himself. It was his presence in the house that had moved his aunts from their garden on Fifth Avenue to Rome. Was it possible that the force tearing them back to 1973 had something to do with him?

Fulcho's clickety-clack across the wooden floor made him laugh, and he realized the absurdity of his supposings.

"Hey, Fulcho," he called. "I've come to the conclusion it's you behind the whole thing." He laughed again, remembering Monk's vow of an eye for an eye. Even the Mafia wasn't powerful enough to get through that back room.

The cat leaped onto the bed, clumped across his chest, stuck his wet nose into Norman's ear, purred loudly and fell down under his arm.

"There isn't anybody alive, with the possible exception of a blue-eyed girl in Rome, who could get away with what you get away with, Fulcho."

And he fell asleep.

19

"I love you, Larkey," he heard himself saying, reaching out for her, feeling only the annoyed response of the hot furry body against his left ear. Next he heard the click of his clock-radio going on. Norman opened his eyes. He knew what he had to do today. It would take a lot of doing, but it was the only way.

". . . as though it's going to be a white Christmas this year. Four inches fell during the night, reaching a new high for this date." The radio began a medley of Christmas carols.

Norman threw on his robe and walked to the window. Central Park was bleached white. And Larkey, he thought, must be walking alone through the dew-moistened grass of the Ferromonte garden. He went into the bathroom and looked in the mirror, which reflected the worst black eye he'd ever seen.

He split the refrigerator's meager supply of milk with Fulcho and dressed in his best suit, navy blue flannel. Then he put on a shirt and tie and the diamond stickpin. He put his bed back into the couch and straightened out the living room. Finally he sat down and wrote a note:

Dear Mrs. Shomer:

If it becomes necessary for you to open this letter, I hereby appoint you trustee of my estate, such as it is. I've taken my life, but not the way most people think. I've taken it and moved it somewhere else and I won't be back. I also appoint you guardian of Fulcho, whom I know you've always loved. There is a trust fund in my name with several thousands of dollars left in it, which I hereby authorize the bank to transfer to you for the care of Fulcho and for any small luxuries you want for yourself. The rest of my property is yours to deal with as you see fit. Just one request: Please call my brother, Mr. Charles Dickens—collect—at the number below—and explain to him that I've left the world. It'll take a little explaining, I know, but I think you can handle it. Besides, he probably won't be listening. Tell him also, please, that I was going to mail him the second Tiffany lamp—which Aunt Elizabeth gave me last week—but I dropped it and it smashed to bits on my way to the post office. You've been a nice lady, Mrs. Shomer, one of the nicest I've ever known.

Sincerely,
Norman

He put the note into an envelope, sealed it and, on the front, wrote, "Mrs. Sara Shomer—Do Not Open Till Christmas."
He rang Mrs. Shomer's bell.

"Why, Norman, what a pleasant surprise."

"Mrs. Shomer, I may be called away very suddenly today for some time, and I wonder whether you'd take care of Fulcho for me?"

"Why certainly, Norman, I'll be glad to. Where are you going?"

"I'm not sure yet, but in case I'm unavoidably detained, open this envelope in a week."

Mrs. Shomer laughed. "Oh, Norman, you are so cute. Do not open till Christmas, eh?"

"Yes." He smiled. "That's it. Well, goodbye, Mrs. Shomer." He kissed her.

"Norman, how sweet." She smiled tenderly.

He went back to his apartment and found an extra-large shopping bag, roomy enough to accommodate Elizabeth and Amy's hatbox—their treasure, which he had to guard with his life. It probably consisted of handfuls of Indian head pennies and two million slivers of broken crystal. He left the shopping bag next to the door and put on his coat. Then he went over to the couch and picked up the snoozing cat.

"Fulcho," he said, "this is man to man. I've loved you ever since I first saw you as a kitten and you've always been my closest friend." The cat yawned. "I know you're all choked up, but listen. As absurd as it sounds, I'm going to my other world today. And I'm taking Elizabeth and Amy with me. I want to make sure they can stay there, even if it means I have to stay forever with them. You see, Fulch, it won't be so bad there for me. I've always felt I had a kind of tenuous hold on this world, anyway. All we Goulds do—or did. And there's a girl there— Larkey—I've told you about her. I'm going to follow her and hide out until after her wedding ceremony. And when it's over I'm going to kill her bridegroom. Why not? I've killed a few others in the past couple of days. I'll rescue her parents and take her away and live happily ever after. Doesn't that sound nice?" The beautiful blue eyes stared at him. "You think it sounds nuts? Well, it is, Fulcho, but then I can't think of another way."

He put his palm under Fulcho's chin and lifted his head. "So, Fulcho, it's been nice knowing you." He rubbed noses with the cat and left the apartment, the blue eyes following him until the door shut behind him.

He trudged through the cheerful snow-drenched streets. How fitting for his final day in the world.

Even the cab driver was cheerful. "It's gonna be a white Christmas," he said, and Norman figured he would be hearing that a lot in the office this morning.

He was at his desk a couple of minutes before nine, the only employee in the place. He wandered aimlessly around the empty floor until he heard his name called.

Sharon came walking toward him smiling. She threw her arms around him and kissed him. She was about to break away when he pulled her toward him and kissed her again.

"Maybe we should start coming in early every day," she said, walking him to his office, where she spotted the shopping bag. "Bring your lunch?"

"No, that's filled with money and jewelry. I don't trust Fulcho around the house any more."

"Norman, that stickpin—which would look better on me—it is diamonds, isn't it?"

He nodded.

She widened her eyes. "Then I guess you can afford to buy me coffee."

By now everybody was in the office and, with one foot in another world, Norman got on the coffee line and went through all the Monday morning greeting nonsense. After hearing "It's going to be a white Christmas" five times, he stopped counting.

Sipping coffee in his cubicle, Sharon asked him about Elizabeth and Amy.

"I'm going there at lunchtime." He smiled to himself. *I'm leaving the world forever and I have to do it during my lunch break.*

"Forgive my saying this, Norman, but you look a little wild. And do you intend to tell me how you got that black eye?"

He shook his head and smiled.

"O.K., mystery man." She patted his cheek. "I hope for your sake that you don't go to see them much longer."

"Today may be my last visit."

"Really? What are you going to do?"

"It's too involved to explain now."

He must have tuned out, because he heard Sharon saying, "Norman? Norman? Who is Larkey?"

"What?"

"You just said, 'As long as I can see Larkey again.' "

"Oh, my mind is playing tricks. It's a place in Rome."

"Norman, have you gone to Rome again?"

He nodded.

She shook her head and smiled. "Two sane people sitting here. Will you tell me about it sometime?"

"Maybe, but right now I should get a start on some of my letters."

They heard laughter and Brad and Max walked in. "Hi, Norm," said Max. "Have a snappy weekend?"

Brad held out a Chirstmas card. "Say, Norm, I got a Christmas card from Linda. Want to see it?"

Without a second's pause, Norman punched Brad in the stomach so hard that he fell against the smoked glass of the cubicle and cracked it. Then Norman stood up, grabbed Max and knocked him to the floor.

Sharon had her hands over her mouth. Norman just smiled, then said, "I suggest you take your Christmas card and get out of here before I get really angry." Brad and Max sat on the floor helplessly, staring at him. He heard laughter and realized a large crowd had now gathered around the cubicle to watch the most exciting Monday morning event in Donworth's history.

A rustling was heard and then: "Just what is going on here?" Mr. Perry pushed his way through the crowd, stared around and shook his head. "Is somebody going to explain this?"

"Just a little Monday morning tomfoolery, Mr. Perry," said Norman.

"I want you all in my office in ten minutes to explain this childish behavior and needless waste of company time," said Perry.

"You don't have to wait that long, Mr. Perry," said Norman. "It's very simple. The two jokers here thought it would be hilarious to show me a Christmas card from a girl I was once supposed to marry, the end of a long line of jokes on the same boring theme. I didn't think it was so hilarious, and the result is what you see here with your own eyes."

Perry wound up. "Oh, really? 'The result is what you see here with your own eyes.' Well, let me tell you something, Norman Dickens. I've put up with just about enough from you. I suggest you continue your boxing practice elsewhere—because after today you may have to do it for a living." Several people giggled.

Calmly and politely, Norman said, "We are not amused, as some old Queen once said. Possibly it was *you*, Mr. Perry."

Almost as a chorus, the Donworth staff gasped and evaporated. Perry looked as though he had developed St. Vitus's dance, his eyes bugging out. He tried to speak, gave it up and stormed out of the office, followed wordlessly by Brad and Max.

Sharon stared at Norman for a long time. "Now I know the meaning of the word 'Frankenstein.'" She laughed. "I can't wait to see what you do tomorrow."

He smiled. "I think I'd better get my desk cleaned up. Might as well keep busy until Mr. Perry's blunted axe falls."

"Well, Norman, dear, you can always be a stand-up comic." She walked to the door. "See you later."

Norman stared at the desk he'd known for four years and he couldn't focus. Stand-up comic, Frankenstein, hits people in stomach, sticks a knife into a man's heart, pushes another one to this death. What have you become? he thought. Maybe he was really much better off leaving this world.

At ten thirty he noticed Sharon in the doorway.

"You can't believe the commotion Perry is making," she said. "It's like World War Three in his office."

"I hope Miss Prentiss is in the infantry," he muttered.

"Norman, you're fading out again."

"Sorry, I was thinking about my aunts."

"Do you want me to go there with you? Can I help you with anything?"

"No! I'm sorry, I didn't mean to shout. I can handle it alone. As a matter of fact, I'm going now." He stood up, put on his coat and picked up the shopping bag.

Sharon walked him to the elevator, and as the door opened he leaned over and kissed her. "Goodbye, Sharon." *I'll miss you.*

She took his hand. "You sound as though you really mean it, Norman."

I do, Sharon, I do. He smiled and kissed her again. She was staring at him as the elevator door closed.

He glanced back at the U.N. building as the cab hit First Avenue and stopped still at the end of a long jam-up of trucks, and he remembered all the times he'd been told he should work for the U.N.

"Snowstorm like this could paralyze the whole city," said the cab driver. "Could close down everything."

Norman stared at the shopping bag, that heavy load—of what? Should he? Why not?

With hands poised around it as though close to a flame, he removed the hatbox from the bag and put it onto the floor of the cab. He took off the immense rubber bands, flinching in anticipation as he removed the top. A crumpled old copy of a 1965 *Daily News* was the first thing he saw. Under this, several cans of sardines and a broken Wedgwood butter dish. Under these, some more newspaper. Under this, three crumpled paper bags tied up with rubber bands. In the first bag, in neat stacks with rubber bands around them, was $87,000 in $100 bills. In the second bag there was more than that and he didn't bother to count. In the third was about five pounds of diamonds—rings, pins, necklaces. He shook his head, refusing to believe it. He neatly replaced everything and put the hatbox back into the shopping bag.

Those irrepressible Gould sisters, he thought, living in the worst kind of poverty and clutter—with this. What should he say to them? That he'd betrayed their trust and knew they were rich and all these years could have lived like human beings? How could they live like human beings any more? Weren't their visits to that back room better than anything they could find in another place, no matter how elegant?

He was jarred back into the present as the taxi pulled up in front of Berkenblitt's Bargains. He paid the driver, picked up the shopping bag and made for the house. But he couldn't avoid looking. Peering through the displays in her window was Natalie. She waved at him and smiled. He turned away, walked into the building and ran up the steps.

As he reached the first landing he heard crying and realized it was Elizabeth and Amy. He rushed into the apartment. They were sitting huddled together on the floor of the kitchen, the three cats meowing in chorus with their sobs.

"Aunt Elizabeth, are you all right? Aunt Amy, what's the matter?"

Amy looked at him, but her eyes didn't focus. With no expression at all, she said, "It's over, Norman. It's finished. It's gone."

"What's gone? Aunt Elizabeth, talk to me. What's the matter?"

Elizabeth's face was gray. She turned to him and her eyes looked at him the same way as Amy's. Tonelessly she said, "It's gone forever. Now we're just going to grow old and die here in this . . . this mess."

"What is it, tell me," he demanded.

"We can't get in any more," Amy wailed. "We went in there last night after you left and had such a lovely night and this morning too. And then, without warning, we were suddenly back here. We didn't hear the cats yowling and when we tried to get in again the door wouldn't open. It's locked, Norman! It's locked!"

"That's ridiculous." He swept aside the lace curtain and went to the door of the back room and pushed. He got that same feeling he had the first time—as though some force was pushing back. And the cries inside got louder.

He staggered into the kitchen. "Maybe it'll open later."

"No, Norman!" Amy cried. "It's never going to open again! Natalie told us! She knows!"

"What do you mean she knows?"

"Right after it happened, she was outside banging on the door. She knew! She was screaming, 'You rich ladies are finished. It's all over!'"

"I don't understand," said Norman. "Please, just try to calm down. You got back here how long ago?"

"Only about fifteen minutes ago," Amy wailed. "Oh, Norman, why? What did we do?"

Norman swallowed hard. He knew, but he didn't want to admit it.

Elizabeth let out a loud shriek and fell against the shopping bag, hitting it. Then her sobs were cut off and she peered inside. "The rubber bands," she said very quietly. "The rubber bands are not in the same place. Did you move them, Norman?"

He felt struck dumb.

"Did you, Norman? Did you open the box?"

His silence answered her and then she and Amy let out the most horrible screams he had ever heard, like wild animals.

"Our own nephew, our flesh and blood did this to us," Elizabeth cried. "I told you not to look inside. Why did you do it? Why have you never listened to me, ever? Did you think I was a senile old lady who didn't know what she was talking about? You did it to us, Norman. For eight years we've given up everything, waiting for that day. And we never looked inside this box, never even admitted what was in it. We wouldn't have touched it, nobody would have known. Natalie would never have known. Now everything is gone in our lives but that bag! And you did it to us. Norman, our knight, who was going to take care of us."

"You took it away from us." Amy wept. "You promised and you took it away from us." She reached into her pocket, removed her little ball and threw it at him. Then she fell against Elizabeth and rested her head against her sister's chest.

"Hubris," Elizabeth said sadly. "I told him about hubris and he wouldn't listen." She leaned her head on Amy's, and the two frail women sat still in the middle of the kitchen floor, the silent cats staring down at them from the table.

He picked up the shopping bag and walked out, closing the door silently behind him, went down the stairs and into Berkenblitt's Bargains.

20

The sight of Natalie stunned him almost as much as the scene he'd just left. She stood majestically in front of the counter in a long flowered garden dress with matching picture hat, a small grosgrain traveling case at her feet.

"Why good morning, Norman." She smiled. "Have you come to see me about something?"

"You know why I've come, Natalie."

"Oh, it's 'Natalie' today, is it?" she said as she walked past him, locked the door, pulled down the shade and turned the "Closed" sign forward. "I detect a certain humility suddenly."

He just stared at her.

She laughed her strange laugh. "Didn't you ever hear that curiosity killed the cat? Opening that box was the biggest mistake of your life. And you don't know what you did for me in just that single act."

He rubbed his hands across his eyes.

"Why so quiet? Cat got your tongue? Perhaps a bit of music

will put you in the mood for some talk." She flipped the switch on her little transistor radio and Christmas songs blasted out. " 'Tis the season to be jolly, isn't it, Norman?"

"Natalie, I want you to let my aunts go back in there."

She folded her hands across her chest and said coyly, "Why ask me? Just Saturday night, when I begged you to let me in, you said we'd talk about it another time. I asked you to remember that moment, Norman. Now you think I can let them in?"

"I don't understand what's happened, Natalie, or why, but I know you can, and I'll give you everything in this bag—everything I have in the world—to let them back."

She screamed with laughter. "The tables are turned, aren't they? Saturday night I offered you everything. How ironic." She laughed again, then spoke quickly in a whisper. "Everything I want, you say? I have everything I want now, Norman. All your life you grew up with the Gould manners, the Gould money, the Gould anything-you-want. I grew up with nothing. When I was sixteen I looked just like I look now, used up!" She raised her hand and ran it along his cheek and he flinched. Her chin trembled with anger. "Your skin is like silk."

She pointed to her frown lines. "You see these? My gypsy father cut them into my face when I was six because he was angry at my mother! And that's what I grew up with! Yes, you had the Gould glory, but I had the Berkenblitt curse! It was handed down to me by my mother, and at first I could only do minor things with it." She began to laugh. "Remember that little lie Elizabeth told you the other day, about how they invited me there because my sister was one of their maids?" She laughed louder. "Elizabeth didn't realize my mother was one of her maids for the first two years they were in that house, and she was then dismissed without notice by Elizabeth. My mother vowed that someday she would be revenged. Well, that day is here, Norman. I've waited all these years, watching them from this store. You thought I was a ludicrous old grocery lady with pretensions, didn't you? You'd be astonished, Norman, at what I know, what I'm capable of."

"With all your powers, why couldn't you get into the back room by yourself before now?" he asked.

"I didn't have all these powers until today, Norman. Oh, I had a few, but I was like a jigsaw puzzle with one missing piece. First of all, I didn't know the room was there until those naïve old ladies showed it to me. Then I tried to get in—don't you think I tried?—but something always stopped me and I found the only way I could get back there was by their invitation—as usual with the Goulds. Don't think it hasn't driven me mad all these years. I even tried to get into your fantastic little creation, the Ferromonte Villa, but I was stopped there too. You know, Norman, you didn't realize it, but you had a great deal of power until you got nosy in that taxi." She laughed, then remained silent for a while. "Just think of the heartache all of you could have avoided if your aunts had been a little more gracious to me."

"After what you did when they invited you—"

She raised an eyebrow. "Was it really such a crime? I wasn't the first extracurricular interest Simon Gould had. My mother preceded me. Why do you think she was dismissed? The sins of the mothers, eh? But there were so many others. Simon Gould loved life, and he was attracted to me. Not too many people *have* been, Norman, but of course *you* wouldn't understand that! Well, I'll tell you something else. I knew all along they'd never let me back in. But I also knew someday they would make a mistake, and I tried so hard to figure out what it would be. But they didn't even have to do it themselves. You did it for them!"

She flounced her skirt. "I'm going into that room today and I'm moving into the house on Fifth Avenue and become Simon Gould's next wife. I'll be the mistress of Grandpa Simon's castle! And you come to me with that paltry bag of money." Tears began to stream down her face and she looked toward the ceiling. "After all my waiting, thank you, thank you, Father." She crisscrossed her arms and curled her lips scornfully. "And Norman, my dear, I'll take great pleasure in throwing those sniveling daughters out. But before I leave I'm going upstairs and tell them. They're going to die alone, Norman. They're going to die while Natalie lives in luxury!" Her laughter echoed all around the store, drowning out the Christmas carols on the radio.

"Natalie, please, isn't there anything?"

"Why, Norman, I believe you're not only being humble, you're almost begging, aren't you?"

"If that's what you want, Natalie, yes, I'm begging."

She laughed her Hmm, hmm, hmm laugh. "I don't really need anything any more, Norman. What can you offer?"

He stared helplessly.

"Nothing, right? Right, Norman?"

He nodded.

She gave him the sidelong look. "But maybe there *is* something, maybe there's just something you're going to be willing to give up."

"What? Just tell me."

"Larkey."

"Larkey? How did you know?"

"I told you. There's very little I don't know. Well, Norman, will you give up Larkey?"

He thought of the face kissing him goodbye. "Natalie, why? How would that benefit you?"

She laughed. "Norman, I don't hear you. Is that so much to ask to get your aunts back to their real house?"

He looked away from her.

"Well, do you have an answer for me? Will you give up Larkey?"

He thought of Elizabeth and Amy sobbing on the floor of their kitchen, the two aunts who were once so beautiful.

"All right, Natalie." *God forgive me.*

"God won't forgive you, Norman! And there's more to it than that. You don't get off so easily, you see."

"What more do you want?" He could feel tears forming.

"I want you to repeat after me, 'I never loved Larkey. Every word I told her was a lie. I renounce her. I want her to be abused by Monk for the whore she is.' "

"Natalie, please."

"It's got to be exactly as I said, Norman. Word for word."

He bit his lip and began to chant, "I never loved Larkey. Every word I told her was a lie. I renounce her. I want her to be abused by Monk for the whore she is." *God forgive me. Forgive me, Larkey.*

Natalie laughed. "Now repeat one thing more after me: 'I mean every word I just said, Larkey. My pleas for forgiveness are lies. I never loved you.' "

He repeated her litany.

"She knows you mean it," said Natalie. "Would you like to see? Suddenly he no longer saw Natalie but Larkey staring at him, open-mouthed, tears streaming down her face and shaking her head. Then he saw Natalie again. "Now do you believe me, Norman?"

"Please, Natalie, isn't that enough? Please let my aunts go back."

"Norman," she shrieked, "you've made me the happiest woman alive. You see, I've finally gotten all of you Goulds, and here's the best part: I have no intention of letting your aunts go back and there isn't a thing you can do about it. Why don't you join the ladies upstairs on the kitchen floor?"

I have to kill you, he decided, and he grabbed the large cheese knife from the counter and lunged forward but he never reached her. The knife just fell out of his hands and he stood there paralyzed by her laughter.

"I don't kill so easily, Norman. But you, my dear, you're so mortal." Like stone, he watched her pick the knife off the floor and raise it toward him.

"You're going to die now, Norman," she said. "One more bit of news to tell your aunts when I say goodbye to them."

In his head he heard himself saying as a child. "Somebody please help Norman Dickens, please." And he realized all through his adult life there'd never been anybody to help Norman Dickens. Who would help him now? Sharon? In two million years she'd never understand this horror. Fred? With all his knowledge he couldn't fathom this either. There was nobody. Then, as the blade approached his face, he thought of a name.

"Signe, help me! Please help me, Signe!"

Natalie screamed and it was the last sound he heard.

21

It was icy cold and "The Twelve Days of Christmas" was blaring all around, enveloping him. He opened his eyes. He was lying on the floor of the grocery and she was lying there next to him. He wasn't dead after all, but everything else, he knew, had been real. He edged away and crawled along the freezing floor until he was far enough away to stand up and not touch her. Holding on to the counter, he painfully raised himself.

He stared down at the still figure and he didn't even have to get close to know she was dead. How did it happen? he wondered. Did I get the knife away from her? Then he looked again. The bodice of her garden dress was torn open and dried blood stained its front. All over her neck and face and arms were gashes in her skin, not the sort made by a knife but more like those caused by the beak of some kind of bird. He looked at her once more, picked up the shopping bag, unlocked the door and walked out as the eleventh day of Christmas poured out of the radio.

He rushed into the building and up the stairs, two, three at a time, falling over them until he got to the top and pushed open the door.

"Aunt Elizabeth, Aunt Amy, are you all right?"

Everything in the kitchen was the same, but as if it were frozen into place. It was deathly quiet. Amy wasn't there, nor was Elizabeth. He looked up to the tops of the furniture and under the tables and chairs, and none of the cats were there. The lace curtain between the rooms was pulled aside and the dining-room light was on. Just like the kitchen, the dining room seemed like a still life. No aunts and no cats.

The door to the back room was wide open. The room was empty. Not a stick of furniture, not a ball of dust. Bare and empty as if it had been scoured and bleached. The last light of day shone through the spotless window, leaving a glowing sliver on the floor.

Norman looked down at the bag he still clutched, the thousands or millions that tied him to the present. He was going to make it in this imperfect world after all, because there was nothing more the world could do to him that would matter very much. And if he ever had another happy day it would not be because of the money, but because Larkey had taught him the simple lesson he'd never known—how to love somebody.

Goodbye, Larkey, he thought, staring around the empty room and wondering where Elizabeth and Amy were now. Cavorting with Maria in the Ferromonte garden? Or in their house on Fifth Avenue? Or possibly they were in the garden of their first house—the finest house in London. Wherever they were, it was where they wanted to be and where they belonged.

Norman left the apartment, smiling.

At last he had given his aunts their Christmas present.